THE PENDANT

Between Loves

Book Two

Books by Cynthia Austin

The Pendant Series
Book One: Between Dreams
Book Two: Between Loves

Coming Soon!
The Pendant Series
Book Three: Between Worlds
Book Four: Between Life
Book Five: Between Death

For more information
visit: www.SpeakingVolumes.us

THE PENDANT

Between Loves

Book Two

Cynthia Austin

SPEAKING VOLUMES, LLC
NAPLES, FLORIDA
2023

Between Loves

ISBN 978-1-64540-991-5

To my husband, Robby
If you're reading this, it means that
the book is finally perfect enough for your eyes.

Acknowledgments

I would like to start out by giving a big thank you to anyone who took the time to read Between Dreams and follow Sidney's life into Between Loves. Without you all, Sidney would still be just a thought in my mind. Your interest in Sidney gives me strength to keep going.

Thank you to my friends, my family both in Arkansas and back home on the West Coast, and a gigantic thank you to all of the social media groups out there who have helped spread the word of this book. Mrs. Light at NN Lights Book Haven has been a great help in showcasing this book on their website as well as the countless other bloggers.

Thank you Tina, for your eccentric personality that easily gave me the inspiration needed in order to create Chrissy.

Thank you Mom and my crazy siblings. I honestly never expected any of you to read the book but I am so glad that did. Your support means the world to me.

Many thanks to my editor Tatenda Creed for tackling the not so glamorous part of the writing process. You job is imperative and I don't know what I would do without you.

Thank you to my Beta Reader and good friend, Margaret Potter. Of course I am ecstatic about your enthusiasm to read my work but what I am most happy about is the fact that this book brought us back in contact with one another. Let's never go another 10+ years again without seeing each other again.

Thank you to my husband, Robby, my amazing stepdaughter Madison and my boys Tyler and Travis. I love you all so much.

Last, a big thank you to the team at Speaking Volumes Publishing for seeing the potential in my story and taking a chance on me!

Chapter One

Hospital

I can't explain exactly what the feeling was like.

Falling? No, this was different from the familiar fall in my dreams. Here, I was awake and alert, if only for a moment.

Floating? Yes, I was floating, I was being carried away by four angels wearing dark colored jumpsuits. They each wore a photo I.D. clipped to the front of their shirts with their names printed on them. The one speaking to me was named Gabriel.

What a fitting name for an angel.

"Sidney? Are you with me . . . Can you blink twice if you hear me?" the angel asked.

I closed my eyes but my eyelids were so heavy, I allowed them to rest rather than take on the unbearable task of blinking. I was comfortable, but something began to bother me.

There was a shaking sensation rumbling through my body. I wished the angels could be less rough with me. The turbulence was interrupting my sleep and the vibrating grew stronger. Where was it coming from?

I felt it in my left leg, and then my right. I tried to ignore it and continue in my peaceful slumber, but the shaking wouldn't stop. It was now permeating my entire body, and I heard Gabriel's voice again. He was demanding, but I refused to give into his requests and open my eyes. It had been months since I had slept this well, why couldn't I just be left alone?

Then, I saw a stunning brightness.

Opening my eyes, I was blinded by sunlight. I shielded my eyes as I turned my head trying to comprehend who and where I was. I was in a bed, but not my own bed. This bed had wheels, and it was moving.

There was a woman down by my feet holding both of my shoes.

"Sidney. Welcome back." She smiled warmly at me.

A young man to my right responded. He held a bag of fluid above his head with one hand and with the other he gripped my floating bed which I now realized was a hospital gurney.

"Her seizures have subsided," the woman holding my feet told the man who appeared to be in charge.

"That's great news. Sidney, do you know where you are?" the man asked.

I glanced down at his shirt and read his name badge: Gabriel.

I heard more shouts and I twisted my head to follow the noise. I let out a wail. The sudden movement hurt. A lot.

"Try not to move," the older man instructed.

"Sid!" Ray shouted.

Ignoring the man's directions, I whirled around and caught sight of my boyfriend breaking through yellow police tape and running up to my bed. Upon seeing his face, the memories shot back into my brain.

Ray gripped my hand and began walking with the crew of EMTs next to my hospital bed. I was being rolled out of Granny's backyard and toward an ambulance that was waiting at the end of the driveway. I squeezed Ray's hand tightly and tried to force out a smile of reassurance, but it proved to take too much energy.

I felt something wet and sticky in my hand. Letting go of Ray, I turned my palm over to inspect it and was surprised to see it was stained red. I looked at Ray for an explanation and that's when I noticed it; there was a great deal of blood on his shirt and his hands.

"Samjaza. I should have known it was you."

Everyone in the garden knew him as the Snake because of the form he so often took, but his given name was Samjaza. He lived in a mud hut along the forest line and filled his hut with the carcasses of dead animals and decaying tree roots. He did not keep these beings for their meats and furs like most hunters, but instead collected them to be used in séances, magical potions and other sacrilegious activities.

Most of the people in the garden believed Samjaza to be an old man who had simply gone mad. But there were still a few who believed the wizard practiced the dark arts and was truly to be feared.

Under normal conditions, Samael stayed clear of Samjaza, and avoided the possible evil that he possessed. But at this moment in time, Samael hoped that just maybe he harbored a bit of magic in his old mind, and an ability to bring the woman he loved back to him.

Samael was desperate and willing to try anything to be reunited with his lady.

"Tell me, Samjaza, did my father send you after me?"

"I work for no one," replied the spiritually dark man, "I came because I knew you to be in trouble."

Samael looked away and turned his attention back to his studies. The two weeks were almost up and Samael was no closer to finding a way out of the Garden than he was the night his father brought down his verdict. He did not have time to entertain the enigmatic riddles of this loopy old man.

"The books you study will not give you the answers you seek."

Samael bristled. "You know nothing of what I seek."

"You need a way out of the gates. The answer is not in a book, but in the dagger you carry on your belt loop."

Samael gripped his large knife and looked into the eyes of the wicked man. "How do you know so much?"

"'Tis my job. I search for those who need my help, and I offer it. Shall I offer the same to you?"

Samael was well aware of the help the Snake offered people. If the rumors of his magic were true, then this man was not a creation of God but rather the opposite.

Samjaza was pure evil, but how could Samael refuse what he was offering? He was running out of time and Eve was to be wed in less than three days. He could not afford to turn the Snake away now.

"What price shall it cost?" Samael nervously inquired.

"For now, it shall cost the love of your sister. Later, there will be another price to pay, but we needn't discuss it at present."

Samael shook his head. He would do anything if he knew it would bring him to Eve. But harming his dear sister was out of the question. "I could never harm her."

"Not even for Eve?" the Snake leered.

Samael sat and pondered this question. He made a promise to Eve that he would devote his life to finding her again, but he could not sacrifice his sister. She was the only one he had ever loved besides Eve.

"I will find another way," he answered. "Thank you anyway for your help, kind sir." With that he bowed gracefully, gathered his books, and began to depart.

The Snake proffered, "What if I was to tell you your dear sister has already betrayed your trust?"

"I shan't believe it."

Frozen in his steps by anger, he clenched his fists and felt the uncontrollable rage he had felt the day his father announced his plans of keeping him from Eve.

"You've suspected it all along, Samael. In your heart, you know I speak the truth."

"How do you know my name?"

"I know all, including the actions of your sister. 'Twas her who spied you with Eve in the forest that day and 'twas her that ran to your father and revealed to him your affairs."

Samael stood as still as a statue as he allowed every feeling of anger, betrayal, and resentment enter into his being and sadly come to rest in his bones. This family he had been cursed with had turned out to be no family at all. Even his sister, whom he felt was the only one that understood him, had betrayed him. He had no one in this land to turn to. Samael was alone with not one friend.

He looked at the old man, and in a cold, detached voice, he sadly nodded his pledge. "I shall do it. My ties to my sister shall be severed the next time I see her . . . provided you allow a way out of this hell for me and guide me to my Eve."

Samjaza exclaimed, "We have a deal."

The Snake then instructed Samael that the gate would open once he completed all deeds required.

The first would be his sister; he needed to sever their bond by blood.

Chapter Three

Empty With You

When I opened my eyes, the first thing I saw was Ray. He was hunched over my bed with his head resting in my lap. He was sleeping soundly.

I looked around at my surroundings and became aware I was in a hospital room. Reaching up, I touched my head as I winced in pain. My fingers traced along the tiny pinpoints running along my hairline.

Stitches. More than a few too.

Lying back on my pillow, I closed my eyes. I was exhausted but going back to sleep wouldn't help when these dreams were coming at me full force. I wondered if maybe the doctor could prescribe a medication that would lift my spirits and keep me awake at the same time.

Ray stirred next to me. His heavy lids lifted and his blue eyes beamed at me. "Sid, you're awake," he mumbled as he sat up. He lifted his white hat and scratched his head. "How do you feel?"

I took his hand and pulled him onto me. He looked like he could use the bed more than me. He wrapped his arms around me and I nestled my head next to his chest, feeling the warmth of his body surround me. He smelled so good, like soap and cologne and . . . Ray.

"I'm so tired," I yawned.

"You've been asleep for nearly 24 hours."

I looked at him with lazy puppy dog eyes. "It felt like I was just napping. Every time I closed my eyes I had those overwhelming dreams. Do you think Dr. Kyle would give me something to help me sleep better?"

Ray looked at me in disbelief. "Sid, somebody just came into your backyard and smashed your face in with a shovel and you're worried about getting a good night's rest?"

He lay there ashen and more than a little shaken, trying to hide his fear from me, but I knew him too well and that look on his face brought me back to that day in my backyard.

I recalled the hazy image of him walking alongside my hospital gurney, his shirt and hands covered in blood. I was horrified at the memory. "Was that all my blood?"

Ray climbed out of the bed and walked to the window. He kept his back to me so I couldn't see his face.

"Ray, where did all of that blood come from?" I brought my hand to my face and felt the stitches again. From what I could feel, it didn't seem like that many sutures. Surely all of that blood couldn't have escaped from *me*.

Ignoring my question, Ray turned around and headed for the door. "The police are waiting in the hall. They asked to speak to you as soon as you woke up. I'll be back when they're done."

"Ray!" I yelled but he continued through the door, leaving me alone and confused.

A heavyset man wearing a black police uniform entered the room. He had strawberry blond hair and a round face.

"Sidney Sinclair? I'm Detective Albright with the Homicide unit."

My mind picked up on the key word in his sentence.

Homicide? Why would the Homicide Department need to speak with me?

I weakly smiled up at him, "Isn't it obvious I'm not dead?"

Ignoring my logic, the detective took out a yellow notepad and pen from his front pocket and seated himself in the chair across from my bed.

"So your boyfriend didn't tell you about his discovery then?"

I swallowed hard and shook my head.

Thinking of Ray, I remembered the way he looked both in the back-yard and in the ambulance, then again just a few moments ago in the hospital bed with me. He had looked so shaken—I had never seen him that scared before.

But what was most unsettling were his eyes. They were cold and emotionless as he attempted to shield himself from what he'd seen. Those blue oceans were now a heavy pool of emptiness.

"There was so much blood," I recalled out loud. "It was on his shirt and his hands. Was that all from me?"

Again the detective ignored my question as he jotted down notes in his yellow notepad. As the seconds crept by, the detective finally spoke and what he said shocked me beyond anything I had ever heard in my life.

"The blood belonged to your grandmother's nurse. She was found dead inside of the home. Blunt force trauma to the head. Do you recall any details during the moments prior to your injuries?"

"Nouri's dead?" I wailed, unable to contain my sobs.

The way the detective told me was so cold, unsettling, and unfeel-ing. He dismissed her death as if she was nothing more than an immi-grant nurse to some elderly woman on her way out of this world. Nouri was so much more than just my grandmother's nurse, she was my friend. She was my *family*.

"Oh my God," I cried. The tears poured from my eyes and my head began to throb.

"Sidney." The unemotional cop continued, "I need you to focus here while I ask you these questions. Is there anything you remember that can assist us with our investigation?"

I shook my head as I reached over to the bedside table and took a piece of tissue. "No. I don't know who was in the backyard with me. One minute I was planting some flowers and the next, someone was bringing down a shovel on me. That's the last thing I remember."

I brought my knees up to my chest and sobbed loudly into my tissue. My beloved Nouri was gone.

"Well, whoever it was, whacked you pretty good with that shovel, and then proceeded into the house to attack the nurse. You're lucky to be alive, Sidney. It appears you were their target."

I blinked in surprise and brushed the tears away with the back of my hand. Every bone in my body seemed to be vibrating like a semi-truck crossing a drawbridge. All I could think about was my mother's warning.

It was just a foolish dream, Sidney. Your mother can't communicate with you from beyond the grave.

"If they wanted me dead, they could have very well killed me in the backyard."

He nodded laconically. "You're right. They could have. But I don't believe that was their intent. They wanted to send you some kind of warning. Your boyfriend found a note on the kitchen table. It was addressed to you."

The detective reached into his pocket and pulled out a zip lock bag. Handing it to me, I turned it over to find a handwritten note sealed inside. It read:

Sidney,
Stay where you belong. Next time it might be Granny.

My hands began to tremble as I read those sinister words. I understood exactly what the person was demanding. Nouri died because I had planned to leave Noddington Heights on Friday. The note clearly said, "stay where you belong . . ."

Slowly my mind began to creep into a terrifying space as I pictured Granny lying helpless and alone in her bed.

"Granny," I whispered to the cop, "Is my granny okay?"

The detective nodded his head in exasperation as I detoured his thoughts and ran him off-track of the subject at hand.

"She's fine. Do you have any idea what this note means?"

I slowly handed the zip lock bag back to Detective Albright and nodded my head. "Yes," I whispered as the tears slid down my cheeks and my heart broke all over again. "Nouri agreed to stay here and take care of my granny full time while I moved to Los Angeles with my boyfriend, Ray. Whoever wrote that note clearly doesn't want me to go."

"How many people knew you were moving?"

"I told my best friend, Chrissy Kyle. Then of course, Ray, and . . . that's it."

I didn't know why, but I decided not to tell Detective Albright about Adrian. It would just get back to Ray and cause problems. Besides, it's not like Adrian would hurt me.

But *who* would?

Just as I thought about her, the detective asked, "Your boyfriend Ray. Does he have any jealous ex-girlfriends that may feel threatened by you moving in with him?"

I swallowed hard and nodded my head. The detective waited for me to elaborate. "Yes, Lilly Lavelle. You'd have to talk to Ray about her, though. He tells me he no longer has any contact with her."

The detective displayed no intention of moving and continued to stare at me, pen in hand. "But you're not buying it, are you? You suspect he's still in contact with her?"

I was beginning to see why this man decided to go into this line of work. Detective Albright nailed it, but I didn't want to allow him the satisfaction of being right. Or maybe I just wanted to remain blind to my hopeless situation.

"I don't know, Detective. My boyfriend says he's ended the relationship and I believe him."

The detective wrote down a few more notes before standing. "Okay, Ms. Sinclair. Thank you very much for your time. If we get any leads, I'll be sure to contact you."

After the police left I stared at the doorway waiting for Ray to come back. That's when the blonde princess strolled through the doors. Even in the wake of a tragedy, Chrissy looked as if she'd just stepped out of the summer edition of a Victoria's Secret catalog, wearing a blue halter top and white shorts.

"Sidney. Oh my God, what happened?"

She gripped my hands, and despite my anger with her earlier, my happiness outweighed the more primitive emotion. Besides, this was a time for healing, not hurtful feelings.

"Chrissy, I'm so glad you're here."

She frowned. "Your head looks awful. I hope that doesn't leave a scar. Who would do this to you?"

Pushing away the ominous warning my dead mother gave me in my last dream, I answered with the next logical explanation. "It had to be Lilly."

Once I said it, I knew she wasn't buying it. She raised one eyebrow as she looked at me skeptically. "Ray's little play thing back in L.A.? Why?"

"Whoever did this left a note threatening if I left with Ray, they would kill Granny. Whoever did this wanted to stop me from leaving.

It had to be Lilly," I reasoned. "If Ray was still sleeping with her, then of course she wouldn't want me going back to L.A."

Chrissy shrugged her shoulders, "Well yeah, but he's not. How would she even know about you moving back with Ray or where you live, for that matter? She wouldn't."

"Unless Ray was still talking to her," I pushed back, fighting hard to make Chrissy see my reasoning.

It had to be Lilly, because the only other answer I could come up with left me thinking I belonged in a nut house. I couldn't let go of my mother's warning.

Samael's coming for you, Sidney. Don't let the dreams or his charm fool you. It's all lies.

Chrissy still wasn't convinced. "It doesn't make sense, Sidney. Why would Ray come home and spend all of this time begging you to come back just to throw it all away again? He may be an ass, but he's not an idiot. Who else knew you were leaving?"

Besides Chrissy, Adrian was the only one I told. I didn't want my best friend to jump to any conclusions, but I couldn't lie to her, either. I decided to tell Chrissy about Adrian.

"Do you remember Green Eyes McGee from the bar?"

"Um, the guy that finally made you realize there are way hotter guys than Ray out there? How can I forget?"

Ignoring Chrissy's crudeness, I continued. "The night of my birthday, after I left the bar I met up with him. We hung out pretty late and when I got home, Ray was there. We fought. I tried to break up with him, and long story short, we made up and then Ray made me promise I wouldn't see Adrian again."

"Okay, back up. I don't want the short story, gimme the long drawn out, point to point novel. Beginning with Adrian?"

"That's green-eyed guy's name. Anyway, I promised I wouldn't see him but I didn't keep my word. I saw him again and we spent last Sunday together."

"Did you sleep with him?" Chrissy blurted out, her eyes as big as half-dollars, gleaming with excitement.

"Of course not, Chrissy, I barely know the guy!"

She shrugged nonchalantly and waved her hand, telling me to go on.

"So on Sunday, I told him I was moving and that we wouldn't be able to see each other again. Like I said, I hardly know the guy. It's not like he's going to hit me over the head with a shovel, kill my nurse, and leave a threatening note just to keep me here. He hardly blinked when I told him I was leaving."

"And you didn't tell anyone else?" Chrissy pressed.

"Just you."

"Oh my gosh, so do you think that detective is going to put my name on his white board back at the police headquarters and I'm going to have to answer all of these questions to prove I'm not a suspect?"

It never failed. Chrissy always found a way to make every crisis about her; she was a complete narcissist. I rolled my eyes in response to her police academy scenario and she rambled on.

"Well, if I had to bet between myself, Adrian or Lilly, I'd put Daddy's money on Adrian." She took a seat and began thumbing through a magazine that had been left in the room from the last visitors, "It's just weird how that guy always appears when you're by yourself. If he's got nothing to hide then he should come around in public. Maybe I'd like to meet Mr. Hottie Pants."

"Did I mention he's a lawyer in training?"

If Chrissy's eyes were the size of half dollars before, they were manhole covers now. I swear I could almost see dollar signs flashing in them.

"Back off," I warned, "I saw him first."

Chrissy scrunched her nose and stuck her tongue out at me. "No fair. I saw that necklace first but you still swooped in and now it never leaves your neck. So what if you saw Perry Mason first? You have a boyfriend while I'm single and ready to mingle."

I tossed my pillow at her and we both burst into hysterical laughter. "Perry Mason? Really?"

She shrugged, "I couldn't think of any other lawyer names."

Seeping back into the serious tone of our murderous reality, I began racking my brain, trying to figure out who was responsible for Nouri's death. I didn't want to hear any more of Chrissy's speculations. To suspect Adrian was the dumbest thing I had heard all day. Lilly was the obvious suspect, it had to be her.

But then if it was her, that would mean admitting Ray was *still* communicating with her.

A chilling thought escaped my lips. "What if it was Ray?"

"Come again?" Chrissy was now applying a thick coat of perfumed lotion to her already perfect legs.

"Ray was the one who found me. He found Nouri, and he found the note. He was covered in blood, Chrissy, I saw him." I frantically looked over at the hospital door, making sure Ray didn't enter.

"Why would Ray hit you with a shovel?" She snapped the lid shut on the bottle of lotion and tossed it back into her beach bag.

"To stop me from moving in with him," I rationalized. "He didn't sound happy when I told him Nouri suggested I go back home with him."

16

"I don't know, Sidney. That sounds a little far-fetched, don't you think?"

"Oh, but it makes perfect sense for you to accuse a guy you've never even met?" I lashed out.

"Yeah, because I *have* met Ray, and even though I don't like him, he's not a freaking murderer! What kind of medication are you on? You're talking like a crazy person."

The hospital door opened and Dr. Kyle stepped in. "Hello, Sidney. Chrissy."

"Hi, Daddy," Chrissy sung in a slow, boring tune.

"Sidney. You took quite a hit to your head yesterday. How do you feel?"

"I feel okay, Dr. Kyle, just anxious to get home."

He took a small flashlight from his coat pocket and shined it in my eyes. "Everything looks good. I'd like to keep you overnight for observation and you can leave on Wednesday morning. I'll write you a prescription for your pain and then I need you to sign a few release forms. I can arrange for the hospital to assign a new nurse to your grandmother's case."

My breath caught on his last words. Everyone here seemed to speak of Nouri as nothing more than a second thought. To them, she was just a nurse that could easily be replaced.

But to me, she was a friend, and it seemed I would be grieving for her alone.

"Daddy," Chrissy hesitantly interrupted, "I was thinking I could help Sidney with that need of hers. I've just completed nursing school and this would be a great experience for me. What do you think? Could you send a referral for me to be Emmy's new nurse?"

Dr. Kyle was not impressed by the idea but as usual, he seldom told Chrissy no. "I suppose that would be a decision Sidney would need to make."

Pushing my silent grief aside, I answered, "I would love that, Chrissy. We could be roommates."

Before she could answer, I heard the sounds of heels hitting hard against the laminated floor. "Sidney, honey. Oh, the hell you must have been through!" Ray's tiny mother whirled into the room wearing a black skirt and white button down shirt. Ray followed meekly behind her, his hands in his pockets as he looked down at the floor.

I smiled wanly, "Hi, Teresa. I'm okay."

"Ray didn't even have the decency to pick up a phone and call his poor mother. I had to hear about it from one of the women in my church group when I found out they had established a prayer line for you and your grandmother. Once I realized what had happened, I rushed down here. I'm so happy to see that you're okay, darling."

Her tiny figure stomped across the cold hospital floor and she smothered me in her arms. It felt good to have someone with no blood connection love me as her own. Once I felt those arms wrapping around me with the unconditional love Teresa so easily harbored I let out all of the pent-up grief I had been feeling. I cried about Ray's infidelity, the disassociation from Adrian because of Ray's jealousy, Chrissy and I fighting, Granny's illness, and now the most recent trauma in my life; the death of Nouri. Everything poured out and flooded into my heart with a pain I had never felt before.

How was I going to get past this?

I sobbed uncontrollably in Teresa's arms as she consoled me. Ray leaned against the wall, useless. He was obviously still shell-shocked from his earlier discovery.

"There, there, Sidney. Everything will be okay," Teresa cooed as she stroked my brown hair, which undoubtedly was caked with dry blood.

"Mom," Ray said, "the cafeteria's still open. Do you think you can go down there and get Sidney some coffee?"

"I'm fine. I don't need anything." I began to object but then I saw a hint of irritation flash behind Ray's eyes. He obviously wanted to speak with me alone.

His mother was oblivious to his cue but she accepted his request anyway. "Sure, honey. Your father is still parking the car, so I'll give him a call on his cellular and have him meet me in the cafeteria."

Teresa kissed my forehead before letting me go. Dr. Kyle and Chrissy took this opportunity to take flight as well. The doctor promised to start processing all the necessary paperwork for her new position, and Chrissy danced out of the room, heading home to start packing for her move.

Ray walked them all out of the room, and then stood by the doorway until they were out of sight. I watched as my emotionless boyfriend stood with his arms folded across his white t-shirt. His blue eyes remained dead.

Swiftly, he closed the hospital door, and strode across the room to my bed. Taking my hand, he ordered, "Don't tell my mom about the note."

I attempted to sit up, but the pain in my head instantly shot through my body and straight down to my toes. "Ouch," I cried.

"Did you hear me?" Ray asked, now pacing back and forth within the room.

"My head," I whimpered, concentrating on my breathing until the pain slowly began to subside.

"Sidney. I said don't tell—"

"Yes, I'm not deaf, Ray. Sorry, I'm a little preoccupied with the pain." I folded my arms across my chest and stared straight ahead at the stark white wall.

"I don't want to worry her," Ray said softly.

I rolled my eyes. "No, Ray, you don't want her to know about Lilly."

His silence confirmed my suspicions.

"She knew I was coming back with you, didn't she?"

At that precise moment, Dr. Kyle burst into the room, interrupting the unbearable silence and giving Ray an escape to evade my accusation.

"Sorry for the intrusion. I just need you to sign a few papers, Sidney." The doctor handed me a clipboard and I began penning my signature next to every X. "You took a pretty rough beating yesterday, wouldn't you agree?"

Pushing aside the uneasy emotions that often seemed to come with Ray, I replied, "I've been taking a lot of beatings lately, Dr. Kyle."

Ignoring my subliminal cry for sympathy, the old doctor accepted my signatures and turned to leave. "I'll have your prescription ready for you in the morning, and then you can be on your way. I'll send a nurse in to check you out at nine o'clock tomorrow."

"Thank you, Doctor."

Before the old man left the room, Ray had devised a plan to escape our argument.

"I'm going to check on my parents," he said flatly as he walked out with the good doctor.

Chapter Four

Ladybug

The next time the door swung open, it seemed to suck the air right out of the room and replace it with a thick haze that swirled around, leaving me in a state of idiocy. I couldn't help the smile that washed over my face as soon as I saw those green eyes.

Adrian was leaning against the door jamb, waiting to be invited in. He was wearing a gray sweater with a navy blazer. His hair was combed back out of his face, a look I hadn't yet seen.

My eyes followed his hands, which anxiously be fiddled with something between them. He held a single red rose.

"Is that for me?" I asked, nodding toward the flower. I pressed the side of my face into my pillow, hoping to cover up the ugliness of my stitches, but Adrian noticed what I was doing and strode across the room, full of intent. He placed his hand on my head and firmly turned my face so he could inspect my wound.

I was mortified.

"Whoever did this to you is going to pay," he growled.

I looked up at his face and saw the anger as he grimaced at my cut. I placed my hand on top of his and he slowly softened his firm grip on my countenance.

"Yes, this is for you," he answered, handing me the rose. "I felt like I shouldn't come empty-handed, but I also didn't want to make a spectacle of myself carrying a bouquet, especially if your boyfriend's still around."

Adrian scanned the room.

"He's down in the cafeteria with his parents. Thanks for the rose." I brought it to my nose and inhaled. Now I was sure every time I smelled a rose I would think of him. It was an empty vow since Ray never brought me flowers.

"I'd buy the whole flower shop if it would erase that day for you. I'm sorry about your nurse."

My eyes filled with tears as I realized the genuine depth of this man's heart. He was everything I'd ever wanted in a man.

But he's not Ray.

"You should probably go before R-Ray sees you," I stammered, unable to meet his eyes.

I looked down at the rose and noticed a red and black ladybug crawling up the stem. I'd have to release the tiny beauty out the hospital window once Adrian left.

He let go of my face and took a step backward, "Of course, I just had to make certain you were okay." He gave me one last smile and turned around. Without thinking, I grabbed Adrian's hand and pulled him back to me.

"What time do you get home after work tomorrow?" I anxiously whispered.

"Six o'clock."

The words tumbled out of my mouth. "Can I stop by your house?"

"Anything you want, Sidney." He paused. "Under one condition."

I raised my eyebrow.

"Remember when we were in my car and you told me the song in your head changed?"

I scrunched my eyebrows together, pretending to search my brain even though I knew exactly what he was referring to.

"That day at the cemetery, before I pissed you off. You said the song wasn't about your boyfriend anymore. Are you ready to tell me?"

I held my breath until I couldn't anymore, and then I let the words flow out with my breath. "It's that Ed Sheeran and Taylor Swift duet."

Adrian flashed me his impressive smile. "I'll see you tomorrow after work."

He exited the room as quickly as he'd arrived.

I laid back and pondered how Adrian could make me feel so unfaithful to Ray. As if everything I had been doing was wrong up until this point. I didn't know why I had asked Adrian to meet me tomorrow evening. It just felt wrong leaving things the way they were here in the hospital. I needed to spend one more day with him.

When Ray entered the room he noticed something was awry immediately. He stopped dead in his tracks and I watched as his eyes suspiciously scanned the room, narrowing in on my hands and more importantly on the rose I was holding.

He stomped across the room and muttered under his breath, "It smells like fucking smoke in here."

Before I had time to deny it, I felt the beautiful flower being ripped out of my hands. He moved so quickly my brain didn't have enough time to tell my hand to let go. Instead, I clenched down on the stem while Ray pulled. The friction made the tiny thorns transform into razors as they ripped open the flesh on my palms.

"Oww," I yelped in pain as I looked down at my hand to inspect my wounds. Ray hardly noticed the red stream flowing from my palm. He was too busy shoving the flower into the medical waste bin as though it were some sort of toxic hazard to our relationship. I brought my hand to my mouth and pressed my tongue against the wound, hoping to stop the bleeding, not to mention the violent words I wanted to scream at Ray. I looked down at the white bed sheet and noticed the tiny ladybug frozen in place. I brought my finger down so the little insect could crawl onto it but it was no use. The bug was dead. Ray had killed it just like he was killing our love.

He snarled, "I thought we agreed you wouldn't see him again, Sid?"

The lingering smell of cigarettes made it impossible for me to deny that Adrian was here.

"Ray, I'm in the freaking hospital. It's not like I called him and asked him on a date. He heard what happened and came to check on my well-being. That's it."

My seething boyfriend stood in the middle of the room in silence.

"Why don't you like him? You've never even met him," I continued, becoming more and more agitated.

"Because he's after my girl."

I flicked the ladybug's carcass off the sheet and stuffed my face into the oversized pillow and closed my eyes. At least Ray admitted his real issue with Adrian and didn't try to hide behind his stupid anti-smoking beliefs.

"I'm too tired for this. Let's just go to bed so we can go home tomorrow."

I felt Ray's warmth as he climbed into the hospital bed and secured me in his embrace, holding me slightly tighter than he normally did.

Chapter Five

Into My Web

I woke up the next morning to a nurse calling my name.

"Miss Sinclair, your boyfriend already took care of filling your prescription this morning so all I need you to do is sign this last discharge paper and you're free to go," the young auburn-haired caregiver babbled.

After Lilly, I'd acquired a prejudice against redheaded women and wanted them kept as far away from Ray as possible. But this girl was far from a threat. She was mousy, with brown, doughy eyes and a plump, freckled face. She looked more like a Cabbage Patch Kid than a human being.

I signed the papers and scanned the room for Ray. He was missing.

Following my eyes, the nurse answered my unspoken question. "Your boyfriend is outside taking a business call. It must be so cool to be with someone famous like Ray Ryker."

The stars in her eyes twinkled, reminding me the Cabbage Babe was indeed a real human girl.

"Yeah, it's a blast," I said as I handed her the clipboard. She was too lost in her own fantasy to hear the sarcasm dripping from my voice.

"He brought a change of clothes for you this morning," she went on, pointing to a bag printed with the name of one of Chrissy's favorite stores. It was very expensive. "What a dream. You are so lucky, Miss Sinclair."

The smile cemented on her face made me want to puke.

I was so lucky because my boyfriend liked to use his limitless credit card to buy me clothes, hoping it would be enough for me to forget about his affair. I snatched the bag and headed into the restroom to see what Ray would like his Barbie to wear today.

My new sundress was a strapless piece of fabric with a denim vest. Ray accessorized it with teal platform pumps that I was willing to bet would be less comfortable than the aching pink heels I walked home in last Sunday.

My anger began to dissipate once I felt how soft the fabric felt against my skin. These clothes even smelled fancy, if fancy had a scent. I was also amazed to find all the necessary undergarments as well as the sundries I would need to freshen up. I wondered if Ray picked this all out by himself or if he got help. I concluded he had gotten help from a commission-based sales representative, which would explain all of the added bonuses in the bag.

Exiting the bathroom, I felt like a hundred bucks. I laughed as I looked down at the shoes, thinking each foot probably cost a *hundred* bucks.

I looked across the room and saw Ray had returned. He was holding a coffee in each hand as his jaw dropped to the floor. I did a small curtsey and smiled at him. "All I need is a sunhat and giant sunglasses and I'll be Jackie O status," I joked as I very carefully walked across the room and took his arm. "All set?"

Speechless, Ray nodded his head as he handed me my coffee and we exited the hospital.

Once we arrived at Granny's, I kicked the teal pumps off and strode around barefoot. Without the added height, I now just felt like a girl in a sundress. Poking my head in Granny's room, I saw that Chrissy was in there giving her a beauty makeover.

I smiled at the thought of Granny being primped and pampered by my high-maintenance BFF and turned to exit the room. That was when I saw *her* room.

Nouri's things had already been removed. Her relatives back in the Philippines had requested her body and belongings all be shipped back to her homeland. There would be no funeral service for my beautiful nurse here in the States. I would just have to learn to move on without her.

Closing the door of Nouri's now empty room, I headed upstairs with Ray in tow. I was ready to down a couple of painkillers and take a nap.

As we entered the pink bedroom, I heard the door close and lock behind me. I turned around and before I had time to object, Ray's mouth was on mine as his hands gripped the back of the denim vest and ripped it off. It was like the scene in a movie . . . frenzied hands tugging at every article of clothing as we blindly made our way over to the bed.

Maybe it wasn't such a bad idea to let Ray pick out my clothes after all.

He was anything but calm. "You had me so scared, Sid. I thought I had lost you when I found you crumpled in the backyard."

Our lovemaking was different than usual. It was as if Ray felt a need to display his strength as he gripped me tightly and poured himself inside me, as if he were using my body as an escape to drown out all of the memories of Monday's gruesome scene. He was rough, burying himself in a pit of sensuality, showing me just how strong and powerful he could be.

In the past he had always been so gentle and soft. He was the only person I had ever been with and there was once a time I could say the same for him. But now he was a stranger with this animalistic instinct that seemed to possess him as he sexually devoured me. I looked into his face and he wore the same dead eyes that I saw in the hospital. No feelings, no depth, and no intimacy, just empty pools of nothingness.

As he climaxed he collapsed on top of me, his breathing strained; he lay perfectly still, wrapped up in his sexual aura. I ran my fingers through his sweat-soaked hair and kissed his shoulder. He rolled over on his side, facing me, and met my gaze.

"I love you, Sid."

The moment he said those words the light behind his eyes returned in bright, living color.

The zombie was gone.

I was so happy to see the old Ray return that I no longer cared about all the new things he had just shown me. I took his face in my hands and kissed his perfect mouth. For a moment we lay together in blissful harmony. The sweat from our bodies conjoined as the tingling sensation in my stomach began to subside. Unfortunately, we slowly began to sink back into reality.

"You know I can't go back with you on Friday." I said slowly, too afraid to meet his eyes.

This had been on my mind ever since my discussion with Detective Albright. He had told me Nouri's death was clearly a threat from someone who meant business. Whoever it was wanted to stop me from going to L.A. with Ray and they had temporarily succeeded by killing Nouri.

My mind drifted to my last dream, which included the not-so-cryptic warning from my dead mother. She had clearly instructed me to run away from this town. Balancing the two, I decided I should heed to the very *real* warning that had left the stitches across my forehead.

I knew it the instant I read that note, but I was still scared to tell Ray. He wasn't always the most understanding when something stood in his way of getting what he wanted.

He somberly responded, "I know."

I was shocked. Was Ray finally coming around and working on his selfish outbursts?

Or maybe he never wanted me to go back with him to L.A. in the first place.

I closed my eyes while I pondered all possible solutions and before I knew it I was out for the count.

Chapter Six

Thank you for the Venom

Samael knew what was being offered to him was wrong on so many levels. He also knew that once he took this route, there was no going back. His soul would be taken, indebted to the Snake.

Would Eve still be able to love him if his heart was now black as coal?

And what of his father?

As much as he hated his father for what he had done, he still yearned for his approval and had hoped to receive it one day. He dreamed of living his remaining days together with Eve in his home. He was still foolish enough to believe his father would overturn his decision made two weeks prior, and that they could all live together in peace as one family. After all, Samael was his only son. His father had made so many plans for him. He did not want to be the disappointment he knew defined him.

But however much he wanted to please his father, he could not suppress his own desires.

Eve had an uncontrollable hold over him. He could never resist the temptation to be with her, nor did he want to. She had become his obsession and he would not stop until he devised a plan for them to be together.

He knew Eve would forget him if she crossed the gates of the garden. Here in Eden, she could remain in her own body and stop herself from aging if she chose.

Outside the gates, however, she no longer would have control over the aging process. She would continue to grow old until she died. Once deceased, her soul would travel through space until it was reborn into another being of her same bloodline. So long as her bloodline carried on, her soul would always have a body to possess. Simply put, her soul would become an incarnation of all her past ancestors, and her memories of the garden would be forgotten. With each rebirth, memories are erased from the past life.

Samael knew Eve would grow old and die if his father's plan was carried out, so it left him with no choice but to fulfill the task Samjaza assigned.

* * *

"If Eve truly wanted to be with you, she would have found a way, Samael," the pretty girl told her brother as she randomly ripped daisies out of the ground and plucked them, one petal at a time.

His sister always found the smallest things to capture her interest and she did it all with the style and grace of a true princess. She dropped the flower stem and pleaded with her brother in an attempt to show him what she believed to be Eve's true side.

"She chose to be with Adam over you. She is engaged and will probably become plump with his baby inside her belly very soon. Do you not think she will easily forget her forest frolics with the King's son and fall madly in love with the handsome, strong Adam?"

Samael watched his vain little sister and began feeling a hint of contempt as his gaze followed the beautiful redheaded princess.

He mused to himself, *Any man in this entire land would bend over backwards to capture the interest of this evading butterfly, yet she insists on following me around with her blatant attempts to fill my mind with falsehoods.*

Before even he realized what he was doing, Samael pulled his golden dagger with rubies embedded in the handle out of his waistband and slammed his sister against the large trunk of an oak tree. Her entire body tensed, unable to move for fear of her skin being pierced by the blade.

Samael brought his face inches from hers and hissed, "Don't you ever speak ill of my love again, do you understand me? I am no longer the brother you have sinful fantasies about."

Her emerald eyes widened in surprise.

A sneaky sneer spread across Samael's face. "Oh yes, sister, I know of the filth that runs through your dirty little mind and the impure desires you secretly harbor about your older brother."

He pressed the knife deeper against her throat as he grabbed both of her wrists and thrust her arms up above her head. She wriggled in an attempt to free herself but instead, she pressed forth into the blade. A small squeal of pain escaped her lips as a trickle of blood the same color as her hair ran down her neck and over the hollow of her throat.

In an attempt to validate his suspicions, Samael brought his mouth to this spot of his sister's neck and let out his warm, heavy breath against her skin. She moaned in delight and pressed her body against his.

"This is why you could not be a good little wife to Adam," he sneered as he put his mouth onto her cut and licked the blood away. He traced his tongue back up her neck to her ear, where he began to nibble.

Slowly, he released her wrists and ran his fingertips down her arms, tracing the pale blue veins all the way down until he reached the upper slopes of her breasts.

His sister wrapped her arms around his neck and thrust her waist into him, harder this time as she pulled his face closer in for a kiss.

"Yes," she moaned, thinking she had finally made him see what she had been feeling since becoming a woman. She had desired his lips on her skin for as long as she could remember. Her wild thoughts swirled in a cloud, lost above her in the heavens somewhere. Her entire body was tingling with an invigorating sensation and no matter how close he was, she ached for him to be closer. She let go of his neck and placed her hands on both sides of his waist, pulling his body into hers. Closing her eyes, she opened her mouth eagerly, waiting for his lips to press against her mouth, but instead she felt a stone-cold blow to the side of her face.

She snapped her eyes open and crashed back to reality. No longer overcome by her brother's antagonizing sexual presence, she was able to regain her senses.

The blow had sent her to the ground. Her nose burned and her eyes watered. She brought her hand up to touch her throbbing cheek. She could feel her face already swelling from the blow. Taking a moment to think, she finally pieced together what had happened and laid there in shock.

"Did you raise your fist to me, brother?" she asked in amazement. She looked up at her sibling who was standing in the shadows of the oak tree with clenched fists. He looked much larger at that moment, almost as big and strong as Adam had been. The dagger was still in his hand and she could see the rubies glistening off of the sun.

"You wicked temptress!" he shouted. "This is all your fault! I should kill you now."

Samael was huffing and puffing in a mad rage. "These impure fantasies you have in that delusional head of yours is the reason Adam needed a new wife. Had you done your duties and been the devoted spouse father promised, he wouldn't have needed Eve."

His sister hissed back, "I will not take orders from that man whom I do not love! He is not my superior, 'tis the other way around. He should have been taking *my* orders."

"In what world do you live where the men take orders from their wives? You are to obey your husband 'til death do you part. You are not to run away and in turn have him steal my love."

Samael tried to make his sister see his reasoning but she was much too stubborn and would not give in to his distorted vision of being happy with that underbred peasant.

"I did not love Adam," she justified.

"Eve does not love him either, she loves me," Samael shouted as the vein in his neck bulged under his skin resembling that of an enraged volcano.

His sister pleaded with him, "*I* love you, Samael! Can you not see that? You are the blood of my blood, we are equal. I am not some dirty little peasant for you to play around with. I am superior to her. It is me you should be with. You should not contaminate your royal blood with the likes of that scoundrel."

Another blow followed. This time it was from Samael's boot. It was much harder than the last but she would not allow her brother to see the pain he was inflicting on her—both physically and emotionally. She sat back up and spit the blood and dirt from her mouth. Wiping her face with the back of her hand, she looked straight into her brother's face.

"I love you and will take anything you have to offer, dear brother."

Samael stomped over to her like a madman, gripping her beautiful red hair in his hand and pulling hard. His sister groaned in pleasure, closing her eyes and licking her lips.

He was enraged. "You are nothing more than an evil temptress and I will no longer play into your twisted games. If you come near me again, I shall kill you with this dagger. Do you understand me?"

Her eyes remained closed, and she refused to give him the satisfaction of an answer.

"I cannot tell if you heard me, little sister. Perhaps this will make it clear to you."

Refusing to open her eyes and continuing to play her foolish game, she did not see when Samael took the dagger and pressed it hard against her left cheek. He quickly ran the blade across her face.

Before she had time to realize what he was doing it was too late. She brought her hand to her cheek but the blood seeped between her fingers. She jumped to her feet and looked at him in horror.

"What have you done to me . . . have you cut my face?" she shrieked.

Samael looked at her with a smile of victory.

"Go on, little sister, run back home and look at your image in the mirror. You may not like what you see, but it will stay with you as a reminder. Keep away from me. You and I will never be together again. Not even as brother and sister. I never want to see your face in my life."

"What have you done?" she screamed, causing the jays in the trees above them to shriek as they flew away in unison. "You will pay for this, Samael. Choosing that wretched girl over me, your own blood. You are a traitor, and a disgrace to this family! No wonder Father hates you so."

She turned and ran away.

Chapter Seven

Alive

I shot straight up in bed, breathless.

What kind of sick dream was that?

I glanced over at Ray's side of the bed as I quietly tried to assemble my thoughts. He was sleeping soundly next to me. He looked so peaceful and I considered this may have been the most sleep he'd gotten in the past two days. I had been so consumed with my grief for Nouri and the unanswered questions of who had murdered her that I never stopped to consider what Ray had been going through and how he must be feeling after discovering Nouri's cold, dead body.

Of course, he hadn't slept well since Monday. He'd been preoccupied at my bedside making sure I was okay. Despite Ray's character flaws, there was no doubt that he did love me.

I carefully slid out of bed and crept over to my closet. Although I adored my new dress, I needed to be a bit more comfortable and so I slipped on some black sweat pants and a soft cotton top. I opened the laptop and very quietly slid into the seat at my desk.

My heart told me to make my latest dream more real and so I began to notate it in my online journal. Every morning while my mind was fresh, I recorded as much as I could remember from my subconscious journey to uncover what it was Samael was trying to show me.

Samael's coming for you, Sidney. Don't let the dreams or his charm fool you. It's all lies.

My mother's warning rang out in my mind before I brushed it off. It was all just a dream. No one was coming for me. I just had to figure out the point to these annoying midnight ventures and then I was sure they would stop.

But I was alone in this endeavor.

The main man in my life was anything but enamored with my enthusiasm. I had told Ray all about the dreams the instant they began, but of course they had nothing to do with him, so they didn't hold his interest.

In fairness to the devotion he had shown me this week, I tried to make my presence as miniscule as possible. But my typing fingers still woke him.

"Are you serious?" I heard him mumble with his face in the pillow. I glanced back and saw his thick, golden curls illuminated by the setting sun through our bedroom window.

Like a compulsive romantic I shushed him. "Go back to sleep, I need to write this down before I forget it." I could hear him grumbling as I tip-toed out of the bedroom to enter my rapidly disappearing memories of my latest dream.

He hissed, "You say you keep having the same dream. Can't you write it down the next time you have it at a more reasonable hour? Who cares if you forget it, Sid? It's just a meaningless dream."

I gave him a parting shot as I closed the door. "I have to figure this out."

He groaned.

That was Ray, it was always about him. I ignored his tantrum as he shouted at me through the door. I didn't bother telling him the dream had evolved since I had met Adrian. Ray would never understand and instead just get angry I had mentioned the name he wished I would forget.

Taking the computer into the spare bedroom across the hall, I sat down and began to type the new details of my dream with the incestuous siblings, more accurately, *sibling*. I suppose during biblical times, that sort of thing took place, but did I really need to dream about it?

Gross.

After typing the dream, I sat back and evaluated my work. Why would my mother warn me about this Samael character?

Slamming the laptop shut, I headed downstairs. It was close to five o'clock in the evening and I remembered I had asked Adrian to meet me tonight. I thought maybe I could leave Ray a note and sneak out of the house before anyone saw me.

No such luck.

As I galloped down the stairs, I noticed Chrissy sitting on the couch trying on my new teal pumps. She looked up as she heard my footsteps. "Hey Sidney. How are you feeling?"

I shrugged my shoulders and tossed a couple of the pills in my mouth that her father had prescribed for me. "I'm okay. Do you like the new shoes? Sleeping Beauty upstairs picked them out all by himself."

"I'm impressed. Perhaps money can buy you class." Chrissy stood up and examined her feet in the new shoes. "I do say they are absolutely stunning."

I sat next to Chrissy on the sofa and looked down at my hands. Immediately I recalled last night's incident in the hospital. Tracing the lines of the scab with my fingertips, I thought of Adrian and how much I already missed him. I wanted to sneak off and see him. I had stated that desire, but now I was thinking of the man upstairs sleeping in my bed. The man who still only saw me as a possession and would never allow the friendship I yearned for with Adrian.

Retracing the lines of the scratches caused from the rose thorns last night, I realized Ray had never even apologized for injuring me. He had been too consumed with getting rid of Adrian's symbol of endearment by trashing the flower.

Looking up at Chrissy, I saw she had already dismissed my silence and now her attention was onto some detective show on TV.

I asked her, "Did Finn ever bring you flowers?"

The sound of Finn's name was all it took to gain my best friend's devoted ear. Although she forced her eyes back on the screen and pretended not to be interested, I knew she was no longer following the dialogue of the show. She brought her feet up on the couch and tucked them underneath her.

"I don't know, he got me a corsage for prom, does that count?"

Ray had gotten me a corsage as well but that was part of the damn ritual. Ray and Finn probably went to the flower shop together to get them for us. I shook my head, still inspecting my hands.

"Adrian visited me in the hospital last night. He brought me a rose."

As soon as I mentioned his name, I knew I had made a mistake. Chrissy had a big mouth and I feared this would get back to Ray. I changed the subject quickly, trying to bring the conversation onto safer ground.

"Do you think if Finn would have brought you flowers you would have stayed with him?"

She laconically replied, "It's too late for me to think of the what if's with Finn. That ship has sailed."

It frustrated me how Chrissy could write Finn off the way that she did. "What if I told you he set the anchor as soon as you walked away and he's still out in the harbor waiting for your return?"

I now had Chrissy's full attention. "Did I tell you Finn was the one who drove me back to the airport the night I found Ray with Lilly? He tried to tell me what I would find before I burst into his room, but I didn't listen."

"I had no idea," Chrissy said in astonishment.

"When Finn tried to explain to me Ray's position, he began by telling me that you were rated a 10." I laughed. "Like, what does that have to do with Ray cheating on me? Nothing, but everything Finn says relates back to *you*, because he's still in love with you, Chrissy."

As Chrissy's eyes began to glisten, she grabbed my teal shoe and pretended to be inspecting the heel again. I took her moment of weakness as my chance to leave.

"You can have them if you do me a solid."

"Anything!"

"Tell Ray I went to pick up my paycheck."

Chrissy looked at me sideways. "That's easy enough. Couldn't he just call if he wants to know where you are?"

"I'd rather he didn't. Can you just tell him I'll be back by seven?"

I stood up and went to open the front door but Chrissy moved too quickly. She stood up and caught my wrist.

"Bob's not working tonight so our checks won't be ready for pickup until tomorrow. But you already knew that, didn't you?"

I didn't answer. I was caught and I knew it.

"You're meeting him again, aren't you?"

I put on my best poker face as I stared at my best friend, feeling eerily similar to Samael and his father.

"This is a bad idea, Sidney. I thought you already ended things with this guy."

I let out a nervous laugh. "Ended what, Chrissy? There's nothing between us. Now do you want the shoes or not?"

Chrissy paused for a moment and pondered my offer. I had found her weakness as she stood at the front door with nothing left to say.

I gave her a triumphant smile. "That's what I thought. Be back by 7:00."

She still didn't move.

"Sidney. You haven't even been home a full day. Don't you think maybe you should just relax tonight?"

I impatiently put my hand on my hip and glanced up at the wall clock. It was five minutes to six. I didn't have time to deal with Chrissy's nonsense tonight.

"Why don't you just stay in? We can talk some more like we did in the hospital and try to figure out who wrote that note. I don't think it's safe for you to go out by yourself alone when there's a killer on the loose."

I knew what Chrissy was insinuating and it aggravated me to no end. She didn't want me alone with Adrian because she still suspected that *he* could be the killer. I wished I never told her about meeting up with him. I took a step toward her and pinned her against the wall.

"Adrian isn't the killer and I'd appreciate it very much if you could stop assuming he is. Or else you might want to look for a new job and a new friend."

I backed up and Chrissy remained pinned against the wall like a poster plastered in a teenage girl's bedroom. Her face was frozen in shock as her mouth failed to work. I used this moment to exit, slamming the door behind me.

No one was going to stand in the way of me seeing the only one who seemed to make me smile anymore.

The only one who allowed me to be myself.

Chapter Eight

Everything has Changed

Adrian's house was a massive Edwardian style home. Shaped like a giant white box, it looked like something that would grace a plantation in Mississippi. The driveway was in the back of the house so I couldn't tell if his car was there. I passed the small walnut tree which was the only object concealing my arrival.

Suddenly, I began to have second thoughts. Maybe it would be better for me to turn around and go back home. Maybe Ray was still asleep and he would never have to know about this secret meeting. But just as I passed the old weathered flag pole, the unmistakable aroma of Marlboro Reds pulled me in and I spied the shadow of a figure sitting on the front steps, his body leaning against the banister. I stopped dead in my tracks, like a deer that had just stumbled into a panther.

Too late to turn back now.

He was holding his phone and he had a set of headphones plugged in.

"What are you listening to?" I casually asked as I accompanied my pounding heart up the to the porch.

He removed the earbuds and placed his phone into his pocket, his eyes never leaving mine. His cool composure was what I liked most. He made everything seem so easy. I wondered if he could sense what a nervous wreck I was.

He looked nicer than usual, his hair combed back and not falling in front of his eyes for once, the gel holding every strand in place.

"You look nice. Do you have a hot date?" I joked.

"The hottest in town."

I smiled at the compliment and nervously shoved my hands in my pocket.

Adrian was so strange sometimes. The things he said to me sent mixed signals. His words told me he was obviously interested but he never made a move romantically. I did enjoy his company but sometimes I caught myself wanting more. Then I would remember Ray and shake those unwanted thoughts from my head. Adrian and I were just friends. Maybe it was better he never made any advances. I may not be able to tell him no.

Taking a seat next to him, I took a giant breath trying to compose my thoughts, but instead I choked on the toxic fumes he was dispersing in the air.

"Have you ever thought about quitting?" I asked impulsively.

He put the filter to his mouth and inhaled, causing the end to burn red, making a sizzling sound. He blew the gray smoke out of the corner of his mouth in a pathetically failed attempt to blow the smoke away from me.

I coughed again.

"What for?" He asked.

I wrapped my arms around my knees and rested my face in my lap looking at him sideways. "A longer life, for starters."

"I'm not afraid of death," he flicked the butt off the steps.

"Well, you wouldn't get to hang out with me if you were dead, would you?" I suggested, waving my hands in the air as if I was some great performer he would be missing.

"You'd follow soon," he concluded as he quickly stood up.

He seemed to be in rare form this evening.

I shrugged off his response and stood up to follow him, but then I realized he'd never answered my first question. Impulsively, I stepped toward him and reached into his pocket. My forwardness must have thrown him off guard and it was very satisfying to watch his reaction as I turned the tables. He was well aware of how his close proximity made me shudder and I suspected he *enjoyed* making me squirm.

Now it was my turn. He attempted to take a step back but the banister prevented him from retreating. I stepped closer and I stared into those green eyes that no longer contained humor.

Could it really be possible I made him just as nervous?

"You never answered my question." I breathed as my hand slid deeper into his pocket. I gripped his iPhone, pulled it out, and spun around to ensure he couldn't snatch it back from me.

He didn't try, instead Adrian let out a sigh as he tried to get a hold of himself.

Quickly going to his media player, I saw the song he'd left off on, the Taylor Swift and Ed Sheeran duet.

He made a feeble attempt to snatch the phone back but my reflexes were faster than his as I playfully stretched my arm up to the sky and out of his reach.

"Come on, Sidney."

"Don't worry, Adrian, I'm not going through your text messages invading your love life," I toyed with him. "I just wanna see your playlist. You can tell a lot from a person when you see what kind of music they listen to."

Now I had his attention. I even managed to bring back that infamous half smile I'd grown to love. "Yeah, like what?"

"Oh, I don't know. All sorts of things, I suppose, but mostly I just wanna see how many songs match my playlist."

Adrian folded his arms across his chest. "Why?"

"It's a thing I do. It sounds a little silly saying it out loud, but what if you found someone who had the exact same playlist as yours, two people with every song in common . . . they'd have to be each other's soul mate or something, right?"

Now Adrian's smile was in full force as his perfect teeth gleamed at me. "So you're checking my phone to verify if we're soul mates or not?"

He took a step toward me, taking this opportunity to regain the upper hand in this game we seemed to be playing with each other.

I wasn't ready to place the ball in his court yet, so I responded harshly, "You're such an ass. I don't know why I even tell you these things."

He was still creeping toward me and I didn't want to get lost in the whirlwind of emotions that usually hit me when he closed in. I dodged his advances and quickly climbed the wooden stairs, heading toward the front door. Adrian quickly followed.

"So now I'm an ass because I think it's weird you're looking for your soul mate, even though you told me you have already found him."

Ignoring him, I went to open his door and retreat into the house but just as I pushed it open I felt Adrian's hand cover mine as he shut it in my face.

Angrily, I spun around to confront him but once I saw how close his face was to mine and felt the heat of his body searing into mine, I once again lost the use of my tongue and stood there dumbfounded as words failed me.

I could never compete against him.

He was the master when it came to making someone feel vulnerable.

"I thought your soul mate was Ray," he persisted.

"So did I but I never expected my soul mate to hurt me like he does."

It was as if Adrian's gaze hypnotized me and forced the truth right out of me, no matter how private the matter was.

"The song in your head, there's a line that says, 'I'll take down all the walls and open up the door for you.' I would do that for you, Sidney."

Adrian's face was now dangerously close to me and his eyes were burning into mine, asking—no *begging* me to make a move. But I was terrified. I was so frightened I couldn't even breathe. I bit my lip and remained frozen on his porch. It had all been fun and games when I had just *assumed* he was interested in me but now he had trapped me against his front door as he invited me into his heart.

I bailed. "I should go."

His arm dropped and he breathed a sigh of defeat. He turned around, not allowing me to see his face. Reaching into his pocket, he pulled out that red and white box, but then decided against it and placed it back in his pocket.

"Can I show you one thing before you go?"

Without allowing me time to answer, he turned back around and brushed past me as he swiftly entered through the big red door. Slowly, and very apprehensively, I followed.

I knew I still loved Ray, but for some reason I couldn't stay away from this dark-haired stranger. Chrissy was right, it was a bad idea for me to come here and I knew it was an even worse idea to follow him into the house.

We passed the wooden staircase and entered one of the rooms on the right side of the foyer. It was a small office with dark wood paneling that ran up the walls. There was a large desk with a computer.

Once I entered the room, Adrian pushed me against the wall and slid his hand into my pocket. I held my breath as he repaid me for the uncomfortable feeling I made him suffer earlier. I reminded myself that no matter how well I played this game, he was a hundred times better. I watched helplessly as he pulled my cell phone out of my pocket and plugged it into his computer. He fumbled around with the keyboard and after a few seconds he unplugged my phone and tossed it back to me.

"I guess we're soul mates now." He smiled.

"I'm not going to L.A." I blurted out. "Ray goes back on Friday and I'm staying. I just wanted to let you know that. Goodbye, Adrian."

Very quickly, while I still had my head on my shoulders, I spun around and headed for the exit. While walking home I gazed down at my phone, wondering what he could have done. That's when I noticed he must have downloaded *his* playlist onto mine. Now our playlists matched.

I told him I could learn a lot from a person's choice of music and he just gave me every song he had related to in his life. He was being truthful when he told me he would take down his walls and let me in. This was his first step.

* * *

It was a little past seven when I opened the door to the craftsman house. Ray and Chrissy were both seated together in the living room. The coffee table between them displayed a half-empty bottle of Jack Daniels.

There was no escaping their accusing eyes. I shot a look of discontent right back at them.

Chrissy quickly rose, her teal heels already strapped onto her perfectly manicured feet, and suggested that she ought to go check on Granny.

I slowly walked into the living room and took my seat in the green recliner across from Ray, his eyes following my every move. I pretended to be interested in what was on TV.

It was airing a reality show about ghost hunters setting up video surveillance in a creepy old building. I snuck a glance at Ray and met his gaze.

Before I could break away, he said, "We need to talk."

Swallowing hard and still pretending to be interested in the people on the television show, I nodded my head. Ray quickly snatched the remote and powered off the set. Grabbing the bottle, he headed out the front door as I followed apprehensively.

Outside on the porch, he took a swig of the liquor before finally speaking. "Did you get your check?"

I shook my head. "Bob wasn't in. I'll have to wait until tomorrow."

It wasn't really a lie. Chrissy had told me Bob wasn't in tonight. I pulled the prescription bottle out of my pocket and opened the lid. My nerves were frazzled and I needed something to calm them down.

Ray took a seat on the wicker chair, leaned forward, and ran his fingers through his blond hair. He looked hurt and I couldn't decide if he knew I was lying or not. I wondered if the big mouth wearing the new heels spilled the beans.

"I leave in two days. I need to know you'll be safe without me here," he said softly.

I stood frozen, waiting for him to finish.

"As much as I wish I could, I can't change the past. I pushed you away and this Adrian guy was there when you needed a friend. I'm not gonna lie and say it doesn't bother me, but I'd rather know you have someone here in this town that might be able to protect you if you need it. You've never given me a reason not to trust you, and I never want to be that boyfriend who tells you who you can and can't hang out with. The night when I got back and you tried to break up with me, I freaked out. I felt like I was losing you and the only way to stop it was to end your ties with your friend. I'm sorry I put you in that position."

I remained silent. I wondered if Ray knew I was with Adrian tonight, but I really didn't want to get into it. Ray had agreed that I could hang out with him and that's all I needed to hear.

I took a seat next to my boyfriend and he handed me the bottle.

I attempted to bring it to my lips when Ray gripped my wrist. For the first time, he inspected the cuts on my hand. He brought my palm to his mouth and kissed the wounds. His eyes met mine and they were full of regret. This was the closest thing to an apology I would receive and so I accepted it and moved on to the next thing that was bothering me.

"Everyone here seems so concerned about me that nobody stopped to mourn Nouri. I feel like I'm the only one who misses her."

I buried my head in Ray's muscular shoulder and quietly sobbed. He wrapped his arms around me in comfort.

"They took her away so fast. One minute, everything was perfect and the next it wasn't. Nouri was here and then she was gone. I came home from the hospital and found her room empty. It's as if she'd never existed. I didn't even get to say goodbye."

By this time I was crying hysterically into Ray's chest as he held me.

He suggested, "Maybe we should go out tonight."

I stopped crying and looked up at him in confusion. Here I was sobbing my heart out over my dead nurse and he was asking us to go out and socialize?

"You said you never got to say goodbye to her. I was thinking all three of us, you, me and Chrissy, can go out for a drink. We'll toast to Nouri and celebrate her life. It's a way for you to say goodbye."

That suddenly made sense to me. I wiped my eyes and smiled at my thoughtful boyfriend.

"Yeah, that would be nice."

He gripped my cheeks and brought my face to his. "I'm here for you, Sid. Always."

Chapter Nine

The Union

Bush was playing loudly out of the juke box when we arrived at the dive bar. The singer was screaming some lyrics about, "wanting to be just like you," as I enviously watched Chrissy greet everyone inside the establishment.

The patrons of the bar were much younger this time around and the girl to boy ratio favored the men. Somehow I had the feeling they were not there to see Chrissy.

Ray gripped my hand and stayed close to my side as he ignored the stares and whispers of the pretty girls. A few of them took out their cell phones and tried to be discreet while snapping his picture.

Dave the bouncer was working the door again, and for the first time, it seemed like his job was actually important since the sexual tension in the place was at a fever pitch. Male hormones make for a combative atmosphere.

Chrissy moved over to the bar and began talking with Jenna, the cute bartender who seemed to be chatting excitedly as she conversed with my best friend. I thought it strange since Jenna usually struggled with putting sentences together. Ray and I walked over and joined Chrissy at the bar.

"Shots!" she yelled. "We're gonna do it right tonight. No disappearing acts, right, Sidney?"

I grabbed the glass and we clicked them together.

"To Nouri!" Ray toasted. "May we all live to be as caring and unselfish as she was."

We downed the dark liquor in unison. It sent a tremble down my body from the inside out as I pushed it down. I couldn't help remembering what happened the last time I drank, and thought to myself I should quit while I was still ahead. Placing the empty glass on the bar, I watched as Jenna quickly scooped it up with one hand and wiped the bar with the other. She flashed me a quick smile before turning her full attention to my boyfriend.

"Hey Ray. I can't wait for your new album to come out."

I rolled my eyes as I considered downing another shot.

Ray flashed his heartbreaking smile and responded, "Thanks, Jenna. I'll be sure to sign a copy and hand-deliver it to you next time I'm home."

I briefly wondered how Ray had known Jenna's name but then remembered he came home late Sunday night smelling like booze. He must have spent that evening here at the bar getting reacquainted with the residents of Noddington Heights.

As she swooned all over Ray, our lady bartender somehow forgot that her main priority was to serve drinks to the customers. Instead, she was intent on discussing the possibility of Unspoken Words playing a set at the bar once the band was back in town. As she and Ray became deeply immersed in business logistics, I turned my attention to Chrissy. She was planning a mani-pedi the following day and so I helped her decide what color nail polish she should choose. In such matters of statehood lay the real issues of life for the narcissist.

In the end we chose red with glitter. All was well in Chrissy's world.

Jenna had been so absorbed in obsessing over Ray that she had forgotten to include Chrissy and I in the drink rounds and as a result, Ray was now several shots ahead of us, not counting the half bottle of whiskey he and Chrissy shared back home. He was drunk and it began to affect him which, in turn, began to concern me.

Finally our bartender snapped back to reality and this time poured three shots of whiskey, bringing Chrissy and me back into the alcoholic fold. But before she left to take care of the angry mob of customers who she had ignored for the past ten minutes, Ray asked her to bring him a beer. As he waited, he began feeling his oats and decided to insult my best friend.

"You really did a number on my cousin, Chrissy. I don't know what he sees in you, honestly."

Instead of being angered by the insult, Chrissy's entire face lit up as she burst into boisterous laughter. "That's funny, Ray. I always wondered the same thing about you and Sidney. Only I don't have to be three sheets to the wind to question it. I ask her every day when she's going to get the courage to get up and leave your sorry ass."

Ray held his ground, still serious, he responded, "It's been a year and Finn still can't see past you. Don't you think he at least deserves an explanation?"

Chrissy was growing agitated. "And don't you think Sidney deserves a boyfriend that can keep it in his pants? Do me a favor Ray, the next time Finn gets down in the dumps reminiscing about our happy little time together, you can tell him that *you're* the reason behind our separation. I watch you and Sidney and thank my lucky stars I got off that train wreck waiting to happen. This right here," she continued, waving her hands back and forth between me and Ray, "Whatever you two are calling it. It is a fucking joke."

And with that, Chrissy got up and walked off. The incident was really no surprise to me. Chrissy always lashed out when Finn was brought up. It was her way of coping with the angst she felt. Before I could decide if I needed to chase after my best friend, Jenna returned. I decided to stay right where I was and keep my eye on this budding friendship. She smoothly slid Ray's beer to him and he handed her the credit card Rene had given him, requesting she leave the tab open. He downed half his beer and set the glass back on the table.

I had a feeling this was going to be a long night.

He turned to me, wallowing in his rapidly approaching drunkenness. "I don't know how you two are friends. She can be such a bitch sometimes."

I folded my arms and didn't respond. I couldn't be upset with Chrissy because Ray had started it by bringing up Finn. She didn't like to talk about it and now that she had finally shared her feelings with me, I understood why. She was still in love with him and I think she regretted breaking up with him. I don't think she believed me when I told her Finn would still take her back.

"What the hell does she have to be upset about, anyway? I have to go to the bathroom, I'll be right back."

He slowly climbed off the barstool and stumbled toward the men's room. I looked at the girls as they made a beeline to Ray once he was alone and laughed to myself at the absurdity of it all.

I made my way outside to search for Chrissy. She needed me to soothe her feelings. I searched the front and the back of the bar but couldn't find her anywhere.

I headed back to our seats at the bar but saw that the stool where Ray had been sitting was still empty. His glass was also empty.

I scanned the room but I didn't see him. I hoped he hadn't found Chrissy and continued to harass her. Ray was *my* problem. She shouldn't have to deal with his callousness.

I headed toward the back patio but then I noticed his cell phone sitting next to his empty glass on the table. It was glowing brightly as it registered a text message.

I knew it was wrong but something told me to open it. I slowly approached the bar, not wanting to, but needing to see its sender.

One new message.

I opened it and my heart sank as I saw the picture of the redhead.

The sentiment was even more devastating, *"Counting down the minutes until Friday. I miss you."*

I read the same line over and over. I had suspected it but now I held the proof in my hand. Ray was still seeing Lilly. As my pain began to subside and anger took its place, I hastily decided on the best way to handle this. I felt like throwing the phone against the wall but I had a better idea. I searched the history of their communications.

I was appalled by the results.

There were hundreds of text messages between them. Worse yet, Ray told her on Sunday that I was coming back with him on Friday. Lilly knew I was joining him in L.A., which meant she could have been the one behind my attack and Nouri's murder.

I spun around and marched through the bar. Pushing past the people in my way, my only focus was on blond hair and blue eyes. I found him outside on the back patio. He had his back to me as he leaned against the wall, once again keeping our pathetic bartender away from her job.

Almost instantly, it felt as if something had possessed my body and I no longer had control over what happened next. There was no way I could be held accountable for my actions. I shoved Ray so hard, he lost his balance and went crashing into Jenna. I saw her eyes widen to an unnatural size when she saw the crazed look on my face.

Ray spun around and put his hands in the air, "Sid. What the hell?"

I waved his phone above my head as I yelled, "You're still talking to her."

He took a step toward me to defuse the situation but the fire had already been lit. Before I could realize what was happening, my arm swung back and I launched the phone as hard as I could directly at Ray's face.

I had never been good in sports; hand-eye coordination was a quality I did not possess. Hitting a bull's eye on a dartboard never happened for me, but tonight, somehow my throw perfectly found its mark. It hit Ray directly in the eye.

The blow didn't stop him and he continued to come at me. I turned around and headed toward the front door. I didn't want to hear Ray's excuses this time. I just wanted to leave. I wanted him to go back to L.A. and never return, allowing me to heal and finally move on from this torturous relationship.

I burst through the front door and scanned the area, looking for the fastest escape route. Ray may have been a muscular god but there was no way he could outrun me, and running seemed to be the only way to get away from him.

I could hear him yelling behind me to wait for him.

I abruptly turned around and asked in amazement, "Are you kidding me, Ray? All this time you've been demanding that I stop seeing Adrian so we could start over, and meanwhile you're still in a relationship with her!"

I shook my head vehemently. "You want me to change when you're the problem? It's *you*, Ray. It's always been you. You're the toxic one in this relationship. If anything, Adrian is helping me see that."

I turned around and kicked my legs into gear as I left him in the dust, something I should have done long ago.

He shouted defiantly, "Whatever, Sid. Run away from your problems like you always do."

Ray and I were like this horrific car accident. He destroyed me, and as much as he tried to fix me, the damage was beyond repair. Then Adrian had come along and picked up the pieces of my broken heart.

He was willing and able to salvage whatever he could. I'd realized now that the pieces of my heart were in his hands. If he could piece them back together, I would be his forever.

Just as I was finally beginning to acknowledge my growing feelings for Adrian, I came crashing into my dark-haired prince. I had stopped at the market on Main Street to get a bottle of water and more importantly get off the streets in the event Ray was searching for me.

As I was entering the store, Adrian was exiting.

"Fancy seeing you here, Miss Sinclair. The forces of nature seem to keep bringing us together." He acted refreshingly calm and carefree.

I brushed my fingers through my hair and pulled down a clump to cover up my stitches as I silently prayed I still looked presentable.

"What are you doing here?" I asked coolly as I walked past him and entered the garishly lit store. I made my way over to the cooler section and grabbed a bottled water. Adrian followed me to the counter, holding up his freshly purchased sandwich.

"My gourmet dinner," he laughed.

I frowned at the battered sandwich that looked like it had been made yesterday morning.

"That looks disgusting." I handed the clerk a five-dollar bill and waited for my change.

Adrian unwrapped the sandwich and took a huge bite out of the soggy mess.

I almost gagged.

I handed him my water and he washed the repulsive meal down. I didn't mind sharing germs with someone as cute as Adrian.

Although I was still angry with Ray, I knew I couldn't leave Chrissy at the bar alone with him, and so I headed back across the street. Adrian walked with me, making no attempt to leave. I thought about suggesting his departure, but then remembered Ray was still seeing Lilly, so I didn't care if it angered him that I was with Adrian.

Besides, Chrissy still wanted to meet him and now seemed like the perfect time for introductions.

We arrived at the old rundown building and instead of going inside, I propped my body against the cement wall and gazed into Adrian's eyes. I preferred to stay out here in the cold night than face off with Ray inside that damn bar.

"Why'd you run off tonight? Did I scare you away?"

I didn't want Adrian to know that his very presence intimidated me and so I shook my head and feigned confidence. We sat there silently, the green-eyed god and the scared rabbit.

"I thought you were leaving on Friday." He finally queried, "Headed to the city of Angels to be your boyfriend's trophy."

Adrian had a special talent for ripping me out of the here and now and watching me crash to the ground.

"Yeah well," I struggled as I tried to assure him that I was in control of the situation between my boyfriend and me, "It looks like there has been a slight detour."

Without warning, Adrian reached out and brushed his fingertips along the top of my hairline where the monstrous stitches were aligned. I attempted to flip my hair in front of my face to hide the eyesore but Adrian grabbed my wrist and held it firmly.

"Don't," he whispered, staring intently at my forehead as he assessed the damage.

Abruptly, the smile left his face and his green eyes darkened with anger. Chrissy had to be wrong about suspecting Adrian as the killer. One look at his face was inescapable proof that this man was not capable of hurting me. He was my protector.

I asked him, "That girl you knew, the one with the necklace, was she your girlfriend?"

Now it was my time to rip Adrian out of the present and send *him* crashing to the ground.

Two could play this game.

He hesitated a moment longer before answering. His eyes rested on my mother's pendant as he spoke.

"Yes she was, but that was a long time ago."

He took the necklace in his hand as he often did when we were together. Turning it around in his palm, he examined it with such sadness in his eyes. I wanted to kiss it away. I wanted to tell him that I could help make the pain go away. We could heal each other. "I gave her the necklace and she said she'd always keep it."

"Well, this necklace has been in my family forever, so it can't be the same one," I said, taking the pendant out of his hand and letting it fall back against my chest.

"I know."

I challenged him, "She's the reason you came back here, isn't she? You said you came here for someone. Was it for her?"

I didn't know where all of this courage was coming from but I needed to know the answers.

"She's the reason I do everything, Sidney," he answered, still lost in his mind, fixated on my necklace.

Feeling I was gaining the upper hand in the conversation, I took a step closer.

"Then why are you here now?" I whispered seductively.

This time it was my turn to get close to him and breathe my words in his face, intoxicating him as he did to me.

But he wasn't easily intimidated, and instead of retreating from me, he took my hand and pulled me close. Pressing his nose against my cheek he inhaled deeply. His mouth moved across my cheek to my ear.

"You ask too many questions, Sidney Sinclair," he whispered in a throaty growl, taking back the control of this verbal rollercoaster.

When it came to us, I was not as adept at this game. So, I folded. I closed my eyes and waited, his warm breath tickling my ear as it moved closer to my mouth. My lips parted, waiting for his to meet mine.

And then I heard someone call my name.

My eyes snapped open to the sound of his familiar voice. I turned my head and saw Ray standing in front of the bar, fists clenched, glaring at Adrian.

I wanted to hide behind Adrian's leather jacket. Instead I just froze, hoping Ray wouldn't cause a scene. But that wasn't our style. Although I'd always tried to avoid making one, drama was a constant when your boyfriend was Ray Ryker.

Ray headed straight over to us, his icy blue eyes focused solely on Adrian, who seconds before was about to kiss me.

He took a moment to glare at me with overwhelming anger and hurt that for a moment, I almost wanted to apologize, especially when I saw the black eye from my cell phone toss. But then I remembered it was *he* who was the cheater, not me.

"What's your problem, Ray?" I reacted, allowing all of my anger to resurface.

His response was a mixture of anger and self-pity. "I guess I finally get to see you for who you really are, Sid. I've loved you since I was fourteen years old and you throw me away like a piece of trash. I can't believe I was stupid enough to trust you."

I was shocked. How dare he accuse me of such atrocities? I was the most loyal girlfriend he could ever ask for. I had stood by his side, silent for months, while he hurt me over and over.

Then a torrent of cruel words rolled off his tongue, spilling sloppily out of his mouth as he allowed each one to lash my skin like the whips they were. Standing tall, I took the abuse. I would no longer give him that control.

"I can't do this anymore, Ray. We try to work through our problems, but we can't because the past lurks in every corner waiting for an opportunity to emerge. Well, tonight it did emerge, Ray. It emerged when you decided to keep seeing Lilly."

I pushed him hard in his chest as I said that final word.

I had never seen such anger in his eyes. He charged me like a wild bull, grabbed my neck, and slammed me hard against the cement as the side of my head crushed into the bar wall.

It took only seconds before I felt the warm liquid ooze down the side of my face. I reached up and touched my face, the blood was now pouring from the freshly opened stitches from my earlier wound.

"I hate you, Ray Ryker!" I screamed, and flailed my arms wildly, trying to make any contact with his body.

From that moment on everything was a *blur*.

I saw Adrian's black leather jacket as he came between us in an attempt to protect me, but Ray was like a wild animal, swinging his fists everywhere. He caught Adrian with a right hook and I watched as blood began to spill out of his perfect mouth.

"Damn you, Ray!" I screamed, lunging at him like a crazy woman.

"Whoa, whoa," I heard a man's voice say as Dave's hairy tattooed arm came between me and Ray in an attempt to break up the fighting.

But I wasn't backing down and neither was Ray. Our fight was a long time coming and we both felt betrayed. We were fighting not only because our feelings were hurt but also for our self-respect.

Soon I felt Chrissy's soft hands grab my arm as she pulled me out of the chaos.

"Sidney. What in the hell are you doing?"

Snapping out of the moment, I froze and scanned the area. We were now in the middle of the street and a small crowd had gathered outside of the bar to watch the commotion. Out of breath, I whipped my head around looking for Adrian, but didn't see him anywhere. Chrissy grabbed a napkin from her purse and placed it on my forehead.

"Here, honey. Keep the pressure on that. We're going to need to get you to the hospital to have that cut reclosed."

"No. I need to find Adrian," I yelled.

Ray shouted back, "Oh yeah, worry about your new boyfriend—who cares about me, right?"

At that point, he attempted to push past Dave and come at me again. It was apparent that he had drunk way too much alcohol. Now people began to take their phones out and snap pictures of the home town rock star as he dueled with his girlfriend in the middle of the street.

Unable to get to me, Ray turned his anger on a new target as he pushed Dave and yelled at him to get out of his way, but Dave was the only thing protecting me from my ex, the lunatic, since Adrian seemed to have disappeared into thin air.

Chrissy ran out and put herself between Ray and Dave in an attempt to calm them down.

"Stop it!" I yelled at them. But no one was listening to me. It was total chaos.

I searched through the mass of people who had now come over to help break up the fight, but I still didn't see Adrian anywhere. Chrissy was in Ray's face and Ray wasn't backing down. Dave was ready to fight and I was beginning to believe all of this was *my* fault.

I screamed inwardly, *I should have never come here tonight.*

Not knowing what else to do, I began to sob and scream for them to stop before the cops came. But it was too late.

I looked to the left just in time to see two police cruisers screeching up to the bar with their lights and sirens in full force and watched several officers emerge from the vehicles.

"Oh God," I moaned, and ran over the crowd. "The cops are here. Everybody calm down," I pleaded.

But Ray was out of control.

He punched the wall in an angry fit as he yelled, "Arrest me then. I'll make bail tonight and then I'm outta this shithole town. Forget you, Sid. I can't believe I've wasted these last few years on you."

He wasted his time on me? He was out of his mind.

A tall officer with strawberry blond hair walked directly up to Ray. It was Detective Albright, the investigating officer handling Nouri's murder case.

Just great.

"Turn around and put your hands against the wall, Mr. Ryker." Ray obliged him. Detective Albright patted him down before placing the steel cuffs on his wrists. Ray turned his head and glared at me.

"Remember, this is your fault, Sid."

"Don't forget to charge him with domestic assault. He put his hands on his girlfriend. She needs a medic," Chrissy shouted.

I pushed her and shook my head, begging her to shut her mouth.

Detective Albright turned Ray away and led him to the squad car as he read him his Miranda rights. Impulsively, I stepped in their path. The detective opened his mouth, ready to object, but I held up my hand.

"Please sir, I would like one word with him before he goes." The detective reluctantly agreed.

I stood there a long time, staring at Ray as words failed me. I was in shock at how things had unraveled so fast and left us in this sad, emotional place.

"You've completely disrespected me in every way possible," he growled. There was so much hate and disdain in his voice I could almost taste it. There was no question I *felt* it.

"I didn't mean it, Ray. I take back everything I said."

Unfortunately, I was a glutton for punishment, a co-dependent waste.

I reached up and grabbed his face to kiss him but he resisted and turned his head to the side. Astonished, I stepped back. His blue eyes turned black as they smoldered with fury.

"You don't get to take those words back, Sid. Your accusations were like arrows, each one piercing my heart. Now it's broken and there's nothing you can do to fix it."

I refrained from rolling my eyes as he pleaded his case of poetic justice. It reminded me of all the times we'd gotten into arguments. Instead of talking them out like a normal person, Ray would run to his notebook and spin his words of anger into another song, one that told *his* side of things and always portrayed me as some emotionless bitch. I hated him for doing that, and again the earlier feelings of my initial anger resurfaced.

I leaned over to him and whispered in his ear. "A broken heart can be mended. But you've ripped my heart out and crushed it. You've done irreparable damage to me and I will never forgive you."

There I had finally said it. I was now comfortable leaving this conversation and walking away from Ray. But Ray wanted to continue our bloody battle of words.

"Your sadness is like a disease infecting everyone around you," he spat.

I shot back, "And your love is like a cancer, invading every inch of my body and sucking the life right out of me."

I couldn't help the tears that slid down my cheeks as I spewed the venomous words from my mouth. Ray stood with his hands cuffed behind his back, staring at my face.

He mocked me, "More sad tears, is that all you have to offer?"

I straightened my spine and stood tall. I had a right hook that I could have so easily offered him. But I knew the bruises would heal and I wanted to inflict a pain that would last forever. The pain of losing me.

"My tears will dry once you've gone. They always do. My life will get better once you're out of it. Just let me go, Ray."

But as straight as I stood, Ray always knew how to stand taller. He puffed out his chest and peered down his nose at me as a condescending smile spread across his face. "I was never holding on."

And just like that, he released me. I was dismissed from his life like nothing more than a roadie in his band's entourage.

Detective Albright placed Ray in the squad car and then led me over to a waiting ambulance with an EMT ready to stitch my head wound back up.

"Does your boyfriend have a history of domestic abuse?"

I wiped my eyes and shook my head. "No. This is the first time anything like this has ever happened. I found out he was seeing another girl behind my back and well, one thing just led to another. I'm terribly sorry for causing any trouble."

"You don't have anything to apologize for Miss Sinclair, all you did was act in self-defense."

I chose not to mention that I may or may not have been the one who started the whole thing by throwing a cell phone directly in Ray's eye.

I was thankful when the detective didn't ask how my boyfriend got the black eye.

"You do realize this incident has moved Mr. Ryker to the top of the list of suspects."

"I understand, Detective, but I don't agree. I told you Ray was still seeing Lilly Lavelle, which meant she knew I was leaving on Friday to come to L.A. Because of her jealousy toward me, I think you need to take a longer look at her."

The detective nodded his head as he jotted down some notes and began taking pictures of my injuries. "We will be looking into Lilly Lavelle as a possible suspect as well, Ms. Sinclair. Thanks again for your cooperation. Now do me a favor and go home. A night out at a dive bar is the last place you should be after what you've been through."

He got no argument from me.

Chapter Ten

Take it out on Me

Rest was the last thing I could think of as I raced past the flagpole and up the stairs to pound on the big red door. Adrian didn't answer, so I continued to bang away. I had to know he was okay, and most of all I had to apologize for what Ray had done to him.

I tried to shake the image of Ray's fist making contact with Adrian's face, and the blood that had spurted from his mouth when the cut had been opened. I put all of my force into the door as I beat it feverishly and finally it gave way.

I halted as the door slowly opened like Moses parting the Red Sea.

I took a tentative step inside, but suddenly became apprehensive. I could hear my voice echo through the large house as I called out Adrian's name. There was no answer.

I picked up his muffled voice deep in the bowels of the house. Stepping over the threshold, I boldly entered the white mansion unannounced. I called his name again but still no answer. I listened quietly, trying to pinpoint where his voice was coming from.

"I said we need to let bygones be bygones. What happened was so long ago. We can move past it, we can go back to how it was before. Just tell me where you are, before this gets even further out of hand."

I wondered if I should leave before he did notice me. I didn't know who Adrian was speaking to but it sounded serious. Was he in the middle of begging his girlfriend to take him back? It sure sounded like it.

Now my feelings were hurt. Was I about to lose *two* men in one night? I shook the foolish thought from my head. Adrian was never mine to lose. But it still hurt just the same. Less than an hour earlier, his hand was brushing my face as our lips had almost met. Before then, he was trapping me in his house, declaring he would let me into his heart, and now here he was asking some anonymous stranger to go back to the way it was before.

Before I had entered his life.

It seemed Adrian was just as much of a liar as Ray. I turned around to leave but stopped dead in my tracks as his voice grew louder. I thought he had spotted me and so I turned around to explain my presence, but then I realized he was still hidden away in a room behind the staircase.

He was shouting into the phone.

"Just tell me where you are, dammit!"

I could hear things crashing to the ground as items were being thrown. "I'm done playing these frivolous games with you. You are still the conniving character you have always been. Give yourself up or I will make it my life's work to find you, and when I do, you will regret it."

There was a brief pause. "Thank you. As I stated before, let's now move on from this, okay?"

Then all was silent.

I stood in the foyer shaking, realizing for the hundredth time I did not know this man at all. If that was indeed his ex-girlfriend, she was obviously hiding from him for a reason.

Not to mention the undeniable fact that he had traveled all the way across the country with the sole intention to find her.

And now it seemed he was threatening her if she didn't give herself up.

My altercation with Ray seemed like a walk in the park compared to this. Adrian's ex-girlfriend was running all over the country trying to escape him. Maybe he was crazy.

Then I had a horrible thought.

Was he crazy enough to kill Nouri when he found out I was leaving?

I should have left the house at that very moment, but good judgment was never my strong suit. Adrian was obviously hiding something and it sounded like nothing good. But did I really believe he could be the killer?

Doubtful.

Whatever antics he had with his ex had nothing to do with me. Adrian was a gentleman when it came to me. He had promised to knock down his walls and allow me in if I wanted him. I was sure all I had to do was agree and he would tell me everything I wanted to know about him. I headed down the dark hallway and stopped at the set of double doors.

Taking a deep breath, I summoned all my courage and knocked lightly before I entered the massive library. Straight ahead were two windows placed side by side that reached from the ceiling to the floor. The remaining three walls housed large bookcases that were as tall as the fifteen foot ceilings.

Adrian was standing at the desk, urgently writing on a pad of paper. I noticed for the first time that he was left handed. No wonder he seemed to so intellectual. I watched curiously as he tossed the pen onto the desk and strode across the room to the far corner. There was a pile of books thrown from the bookcase in total disarray on the floor. He looked over at me but he seemed too busy to acknowledge my presence. Leaning his upper body against the shelf, he began to push the heavy piece of furniture away from the wall. Behind the shelf was a safe built into the wall. He quickly punched in a code and opened it, retrieving an old book. The pages were yellowed and the red hard cover was deeply faded.

Adrian tossed the book onto his desk and looked up as he finally met my eyes. It looked as if he was just now seeing me standing in the library for the first time.

"Sorry for intruding. The door was open. I knocked but you didn't answer."

He didn't respond and instead just stared at my face. I met his gaze, trying to read his expression but he wasn't letting me in this time.

"You've been crying," he concluded, in a matter-of-fact way.

I wondered if this routine was getting old for Adrian. It seemed every time Ray and I had a problem, I ran to Adrian. Had he noticed?

"Come in, Sidney; let me have a look at what he did to you."

I rushed across the giant room. I knew he was concerned about the injuries I had sustained, but I was more concerned about him. I gently took his face in my hands and inspected his wounds. He'd suffered a split lip, but other than that he was unscathed. I touched my finger to his mouth and lightly rubbed it, wishing my touch could heal his injury.

"I'm so sorry," I tenderly whispered.

He didn't answer. Instead he took my face and brushed his hand against my cut.

We were just two victims of Ray's violence.

I turned my face into his warm hand. It felt so good to be this close to him. I looked into his green eyes and for a moment thought maybe I could take all of my anger out right here. I could put my lips on his and get lost in the feelings of this new person. I could get back at Ray that way.

I shook the temping thoughts from my head. I would never allow Adrian to be a pawn in this emotional game Ray and I had always played. Adrian was too good of a person to be involved in that.

He looked at me with a sheepish grin. "I didn't know Ray Ryker from Unspoken Words was your boyfriend."

I dropped my hand from his soft face and looked at him skeptically. "Is that why you didn't fight back when he punched you? You were too star struck?"

He shook his head. "I just didn't realize your boyfriend was so famous, that's all."

I brought my face close to his, the same way he liked to do when he teased me.

"I can get his autograph for you the next time I see him if you'd like."

As I made the suggestion I couldn't help but burst into laughter. All of the crazy things I had been through finally seemed to be catching up to me and now I felt like I might welcome a strait-jacket and a padded room. At least I'd get a decent night's rest.

Adrian sat silent, choosing not to engage in my crazy laughter. Instead, he touched my head and I could see the anger return to his eyes as he looked over my freshly opened cut.

"I'd prefer you didn't see him again."

I took a deep breath trying to keep my emotions in check. "That shouldn't be very hard to do. I'm pretty sure we're broken up."

Not wanting to rehash the memories of tonight's dreadful event, I turned toward the door and began to walk out. I needed to go home, but then I remembered the conversation I had heard moments before.

I turned and asked him, "Who were you talking to on the phone?"

Adrian's eyes got big. "You heard that?"

Embarrassed for eavesdropping, I looked down at the floor in shame.

"It was a client I've been working with. We've posted his bail and now he's fled. You just witnessed the not so glamorous part of my job."

"Don't you have bounty hunters to deal with bail jumpers?"

Adrian smiled. "Not at Adley and Ayers Law Firm. We don't mind getting down and dirty over there. We have no problem playing the lawyer and the hunter if needed."

The way he said hunter sent shivers down my spine. I wouldn't mind being hunted by someone like him. If given the opportunity, I might even skip bail just to have him hunt me.

Looking up, I noticed Adrian must have still been in hunter mode. He was staring at me as if I were his next meal. I could see what might happen if I stayed any longer, and so I turned around and began heading out of the house.

Adrian followed, and once we were on the front porch, he reached into his pocket, pulled out a cigarette, and lit it.

He gave me a slight frown and took a long drag and slowly exhaled, "Why are you leaving?"

That was a funny question. It had to be close to two o'clock in the morning. Did he expect that I would just stay the night?

In absence of a good answer, I shrugged my shoulders. "I don't know. I need to go home and get some rest. Everything feels like it's falling apart right now."

Adrian took another drag of his cigarette as he casually watched me with his calm demeanor.

"Maybe it's falling into place, Sidney."

I rolled my eyes and headed down the narrow pathway that led to the sidewalk.

He followed me and made an offer, "You said if I wanted you to stay longer, I'd have to ask you to stay for a movie or something."

I stopped and suppressed the smile that was fighting to escape my mouth.

Turning around, I said, "I was assuming the invitation would be extended sometime during the day, not in the middle of the night."

"I have Netflix. We can watch whatever you want."

Then he turned around and headed into the house without waiting for my answer. I hated how sure of himself he could be sometimes. As if he just knew I would follow him wherever he went. I had half a mind to leave. To show him that I did in fact have freedom of choice and he shouldn't be so presumptuous to assume I would follow.

But I didn't want to go home and deal with my painful emotions the night had brought me.

It sounded so much easier to go inside and get lost in a fictional movie with my mysterious new guy.

So, I followed Adrian back into the giant white house.

Chapter Eleven

Foolish Games

Adrian was already in the kitchen by the time I'd re-entered the house.

"Are you hungry?" he yelled. "I can fix you something to eat if you'd like."

Unable to contain my dry humor, I responded, "You mean you can make something *besides* a sandwich?"

"Of course. I have microwave popcorn."

While Adrian fumbled around the kitchen, I searched for the remote control and began browsing through the guide when I saw that the re-make of *The Great Gatsby* had just begun. I loved this movie and so I quickly flipped it on.

Adrian entered the room and sat on the other end of the couch. He stretched his arms out so that his fingertips were almost touching my shoulder. I tried to remain frozen in my spot but eventually the buttery smell of popcorn got the best of me and I scooted closer to him and plunged my hand into the bag.

"Did you find a movie you want to watch?"

"If it's okay with you, this is one of my favorites," I gushed.

"Well then, let's take a journey into the mind of Miss Sidney Sin-clair, shall we?"

We sat back and watched the tragic love story that always captured my heart. I loved the latest film adaptation with the bright colors and the current songs remixed with a bit of jazz giving them a reminiscent feeling of the roaring twenties. The lively dance parties were so extrav-agant that I always wished I could just jump right into the screen and participate with the party-goers. Their outfits were so eccentric yet everyone seemed to be full of confidence. Everyone was so happy, lost in a story full of money, glitz and glamour.

The ending always left me with a bitter taste in my mouth; a disgusted feeling in the pit of my stomach and my heart, leaving it feeling sad, empty, and unfulfilled. I was terribly sad because Gatsby had let everything in his life slip away except for his one true love. Everything he had done was for Daisy Buchanan.

I was disgusted by how Daisy could betray someone she claimed to love so much and instead stay with a man who treated her like dirt. I concluded that Daisy deserved her husband, Tom Buchanan but Gatsby, well, Gatsby deserved so much *more*.

His only crime was falling in love with the wrong woman. If only he had never met her, his life would have been so much different.

The film ended in the same way it had begun; with Daisy still looking sad and pathetic in her unhappy marriage as she yearned to be with Gatsby, but the viewers watching the movie no longer felt sorry for her. *She* was the creator of her own destruction.

Watching the credits scroll across Adrian's flat screen TV, I sat on the couch thinking of Tom Buchanan. I thought of the scene when he and Gatsby were both pleading their case to Daisy as they begged her to choose each of them.

Ironically, Tom never showed any interest in Daisy until he felt threatened by Gatsby. She was nothing but a possession to him. '*Once in a while I go out on a spree but I always come back,*' was the sorry excuse he gave Daisy as he was pleading his case.

"Well, if you relate movies to your life like you do with songs, I can definitely see why you would like this one," Adrian announced as he invaded my sad, dark thoughts.

He grabbed a small pillow and lay down on the couch, bringing his head inches from my thigh.

"How so?" I retorted.

He sat back up and stared into my face, "Are you kidding me? Tom was obviously Ray and you are Daisy here."

"I hate Daisy," I snarled, completely appalled that he would compare *me* to that selfish little witch. "Besides, I don't have a Gatsby pining after me, purchasing a mansion next to my house in the hopes of me joining him for our epic reunion."

Adrian laughed and shook his head as he grabbed the empty bag of popcorn and headed toward the kitchen.

Anxious to change the subject, I shouted after him, "It's so strange that you grew up on the other side of the country when your family was originally from here. Most people who grow up here never leave this pathetic town."

He re-entered the living room and sat down on the couch, but this time he left no space between us.

"Who knows, maybe I'll stay in this town after all."

He grabbed the couch pillow but unlike before, he placed it in my lap and rested his head on top of it. Instinctually I placed my hand on it and allowed my fingers to glide through his sleek black hair.

"That feels good," he murmured, his eyes closed.

I felt like I could stay there forever with him. Having him so close to me felt right. Touching him and feeling those butterflies in my stomach felt more than a little exciting to me.

"You say most people who grow up here stay, but Ray didn't . . . did he?"

His eyes were still closed but there was a slight smile around the corners of his mouth. He seemed to enjoy the destructiveness of my relationship.

I stopped stroking his hair.

"I guess there was nothing to keep him," I reluctantly answered, as I came to the conclusion that perhaps my relationship with Ray had finally run its course.

Adrian's eyes opened and he sat up on the couch and stared at me. I thought he was finally going to kiss me. I must have said the right words affirming that his advances would be welcomed. I waited but he never brought his face any closer to mine.

"*You* should have been enough to keep him here, Sidney."

I looked down at the beige couch and began playing with a loose thread, suddenly not wanting to continue this conversation.

"Well, I guess I wasn't enough," was all I could reply.

I looked up and met his gaze, waiting for him to challenge my conclusion.

"I guess you weren't," he agreed.

His comment struck a nerve. It was okay for me to wallow in self-pity and conclude that I was simply not enough for Ray, but for someone *else* to say that to me really stung.

I grabbed my purse and rocketed off the couch. I threw the big red door open but then stopped in my tracks and spun around to confront Adrian. I didn't have to go far. He had followed me to the door. I opened my mouth, ready to lay into him but he cut me off.

"Look, Sidney. I know this isn't my place to give my two cents and maybe I should learn when to shut my mouth, but all I'm saying is, if you're not enough for Ray, why is *he* enough for you?"

I had never really thought of it that way.

Why did I put up with all of this?

I did my best to defend my actions. "Because I promised I would wait for him and be supportive of his dream," I mechanically answered, suddenly realizing even I was a little unsure about my answer.

"And how long did you plan on being his whipping girl?"

Adrian raised his arm above my head and pushed the front door shut. He took a step closer until his face was inches from mine. His scent was mixed with cigarettes and cologne and it was whirling around, making me dizzy with foolishness again.

He emotionally leveled me. "What are you going to pass up while you're waiting for him?"

Of all the mixed signals Adrian let off, this one was unlike any he had said to me. This statement was loud and clear. He felt the same attraction for me that I felt for him.

I gripped the bottom of his brown sweater and played with the wool, pulling it closer to me. He obliged and took a step closer. Our bodies were now touching and the warmth of each of us radiated serious heat. My back was pressed against the door and he was in front of me. There was no escape and for the first time, I didn't want one. I didn't want to run away like I so often did when the situation got awkward. I was staring into his eyes, trying to get him to read what my mouth refused to say. But he was a statue, waiting for me to answer.

"Am I passing something up?" I breathed, barely comprehending anything else in the universe at that singular moment.

He said nothing. Instead he brought his gaze down to my necklace once again as his hand gripped the pendant. I closed my eyes and clawed at the door while I envisioned myself gripping those dark locks of hair and pulling his face into mine. I bit my bottom lip as I forced those images out of my mind.

Friends, that's all, I promised myself.

But then my hands deceived me as they reached up and gripped his face. I couldn't wait any longer for these foolish games. I pulled his face down so that his lips were next to mine and I could feel his breath.

My whole body tingled at the thought of him this close to me. I wanted him so bad. I could feel the tension in his body diminish and he slowly began to give in. His lips spread apart as he pressed them to mine.

Then a phone rang.

We broke away from the trance we were in and Adrian pulled the cell phone out of his pocket. He searched my eyes for some kind of response but I revealed nothing. There was no way I was going to be the one to determine what this all meant.

He looked down at the caller ID and assured me, "It's just a client."

My previous instinct to flee returned. "I should go," I breathed. "I'm sorry"

He said nothing and instead turned around and headed back into the library. Placing the phone against his ear, he answered it as he walked through the double doors.

My heart sank into my stomach. I desperately wanted to know who was on the other end. Whoever it was, they were obviously more important to Adrian than our inexplicable embrace. It also bothered me that every time he got close to me, he always put up a wall and grabbed my necklace. It was obvious my necklace reminded him of someone. It was also apparent he had some unfinished business and he was clearly not ready to start a new relationship until it was settled.

Was that phone call part of that same business? He said it was a *client* but I couldn't believe a client would be calling at this hour.

I laughed at my observation as I realized I was so worried about Adrian's relationship responsibility that I had forgotten about my own. It was easy for me to blame my lack of relationship on Adrian, but the fact of the matter was that he had every right not to become involved with a girl who already had a boyfriend.

If I wanted Adrian, there was a choice that would have to be made by no one else but me.

This was my call all the way.

Ray would have to be completely out of my life.

Chapter Twelve

Saving Us

When I woke up the next morning I felt the full impact of my mistake.

As soon as I opened my eyes it felt as if all of the oxygen had been sucked from the atmosphere as I lay in bed, struggling to catch my breath.

I gasped for air, but my lungs were depleted and I felt as if I might die, right there in bed. I clutched my chest, attempting to soothe the scorching ache inside but I knew it was no use. Nothing could extinguish the flame that burned inside my chest. The fire had burned for too long. I knew there was no saving it because inside, it was just an empty cavity. The burning ash of what once was.

Because I believed I no longer had a heart.

Ray had ripped it out of my chest the night before.

I no longer felt the high of the adrenaline that last night's fight brought and cushioned the blow. Now, I was only left with the dire feelings of regret as I emotionally fell downward into the reality of my personal hell.

I have to fix this. I have to find Ray and apologize to him for the words I'd spewed at him.

It was true; I had become the new poster child for co-dependency.

I wanted to hurt him so bad last night but I should have known better. Ray was invincible and all of the hurt I forced out of my body had, as usual, bounced off of him and ricocheted back into me, causing catastrophic psychological damage. The pain in my chest was almost unbearable and the walls in the room seemed to be closing in on me.

Where the hell were my pills?

I jumped out of bed and ran to the window to check the driveway. I had slept in too late, Ray's Jaguar was gone. Rene must have posted his bail and now he had disappeared out of my life for good.

I held my breath, hoping to stop the tears from falling as I realized I had probably blown my only chance of ever seeing him again.

Sure, we'd had innumerable fights in our past, but none like this one. My insides screamed at me that this time was different. This time our breakup was real.

Reaching up, I touched my re-stitched forehead and realized I even had the wounds to prove it. Just like the song in my mind before I had met Adrian, I now carried the battle scars of Ray and our toxic relationship, not only on the inside but on the outside, as well.

Still refusing to accept defeat, I took off like a banshee, flying down the stairs completely out of control. I collided with Chrissy, sending us both on our bottoms.

"Jesus, Sidney, watch where you're going."

"Ray!" I shouted incoherently. "How long ago did he leave?"

Without waiting for an answer, I grabbed my cell phone and began punching in his number.

"I'm sorry but the subscriber you've reached does not accept calls from this number."

"What?" I yelled into my phone.

"I said that I went to change Emmy's bedpan and by the time I got done his car was already gone," Chrissy explained.

I redialed the number, this time slowly and precisely, making sure I entered every number perfect. I got the same recording.

Unable to believe what was happening, I logged onto my Facebook account to instant message him but I couldn't access his page. There was a message saying the user had blocked my account.

After spending the next five minutes thumbing through every social media site available, I finally came to the realization that this was not some technical glitch. Ray had intentionally blocked me from all forms of communication.

"No. No. No. No. No," I chanted trying to will all of this away.

Using my shaky hands to stuff my phone back into my pocket, I wondered again where my pills were. My head was throbbing as I refused to acknowledge the truth about what was unfolding.

"When did you change Granny's bedpan?" I screamed at Chrissy.

She cowered in front of me, shrugging. "I don't know, like fifteen minutes ago."

I had one more trick up my sleeve before this became completely hopeless. Racing into the kitchen, I grabbed my truck keys and a pill bottle Chrissy must have left out while preparing Granny's breakfast. I opened the bottle and dropped a couple down my throat, then stuffed the bottle into my pocket next to my phone.

* * *

Careening down the street in my truck, I skidded to a halt in front of Ray's parents' house. I didn't see the Jaguar but maybe Teresa would at least have a lead as to the whereabouts of her son.

Taking a few quick breaths and realizing the yoga-style of breathing was not helping my nerves, I grabbed Granny's container and threw another pill into my mouth before I stepped out of the truck.

After I pounded on the door several times, it finally swung open. Kendall stood with her arms crossed, peering at me through her steel gray eyes. "Wow, you have some nerve showing your face around here after what you did to my brother."

I swallowed her insult down with a side of Granny's pills as I screamed internally, *Why in the hell are these things taking so long to work? Go away pain.*

I closed my eyes and waited for the pills to kick in and take me to a place where I wouldn't feel so guilty. A place where I wouldn't feel anything.

Finally, the medication began to kick in.

With renewed confidence I shouted at her, "Shut up, Kendall, and get your fucking mom!"

As soon as I said it, I wished I could take it back but it was too late. Teresa heard the obscene way I had just spoken to her youngest daughter and I didn't know if it was Teresa's look of contempt or the effects of the medication, but suddenly I felt the earth moving under my feet and I gripped the door frame to stop from being sucked into the vortex that was opening up in front of me. I looked at Teresa to see if she had felt the shift in the earth but both she and Kendall were gaping at me like I was Hulk Hogan's tag team partner.

"Raymond," Teresa yelled.

Oh thank God, Ray is still here. I knew he wouldn't leave me like this.

I felt his strong arms as they gripped my waist and guided me toward the family suburban.

"Where's your Jaguar, babe?" I asked Ray.

"Honey, I'm Ray Senior and we're going to get you to a hospital as fast as we can. Hang in there, okay?"

I couldn't get the dopey smile off my face as I closed my eyes and floated toward the suburban. "I knew you wouldn't leave me, Ray. I love you."

* * *

For the second time in a week I woke up in a hospital bed. Only this time, it wasn't Ray's hand gripping mine but his diminutive mother's.

"Teresa?" I creaked.

My throat was so dry and pasty. I went to lick my chapped lips but my tongue held no moisture to spare. Ray's mother saw my discomfort and quickly poured me a cup full of water. I graciously accepted it as I gulped it down in two swallows.

"Are you okay, sweetie?" she asked gently.

I nodded my head, still a little confused as to why I was in the hospital again. Then Dr. Kyle walked in.

"Good afternoon, Sidney. I must say I'm flattered you keep finding ways to visit me, but I'd much rather visit you over lemonade at the house."

I was completely disoriented. "How did I get here?"

Teresa responded, "Ray and I brought you. Have you forgotten that?"

I tried to sit up., "Ray's here? Where is he? I have to see him!"

"Settle down, Sidney. There's really no need to get all worked up now, is there?" The doctor chuckled.

Teresa looked on somberly. "Ray Senior and I took you here."

The way she said *Senior* gave me all the validation I needed.

Ray Senior had brought me here. She had said that with a bit of contempt as if the thought of her own son admitting me would be completely ludicrous.

At her statement, I realized Ray was back in L.A. and that I would likely not be seeing him in the near future, if ever. That one sentence was all my body needed to accelerate the shaking of my hands and the aching of my head. Reaching up, I touched my mutilated forehead. My body seemed to be falling apart, joining my wounded heart in the process.

Dr. Kyle added insult to injury. "It seems you must have accidently taken your grandmother's prescription, believing it to be your own."

Great, now I'm stupid too?

The perks of your doctor being the parent of your best friend, he never suspected I did these types of things intentionally.

"Um, yeah, I must have."

Maybe I was stupid after all.

"Not to worry. Mrs. Ryker found the bottle in your pocket and so we were able to identify the pills you'd ingested. They were just some heavy sedatives so you may feel a bit groggy but other than that you will survive."

The doctor checked his beeper as a page came in. "Just make sure my daughter does a better job separating the two prescriptions next time, okay?"

I nodded my head as Dr. Kyle tightened his cheek muscles and flexed out a smile before leaving the room; inadvertently leaving me and my ex-boyfriend's mother alone.

"Is Ray really gone?"

Teresa tried to be as gentle as possible when she replied that we really shouldn't be discussing her son at the moment but no amount of sugar could coat that insult. She was shutting me out of her life the same way Ray had.

Of course she was blaming me for the entire incident of what had happened last night. I'm sure Ray told his mother only part of the story, letting her know he had caught me intimately close to another man, and conveniently leaving out the part about his relationship with Lilly. I opened my mouth to tell Teresa the truth of her son but I couldn't do it. I couldn't break it to the poor woman that her precious boy was a serial cheater. Ray had broken enough hearts, and the last thing I wanted was for him to hurt his mother the way he had hurt me. So I allowed her to go on thinking he was a devoted humanitarian who had been emotionally devastated by his heartless girlfriend. Why not? I was sure Ray would write a song about it and all his fans would sympathize with the poor boyfriend.

How pathetic was that?

I was discharged from the hospital and Teresa was nice enough to give me a ride home. She never once mentioned the plans on Sunday to speak to Father Renley about scheduling my baptism, so I guess I was off the hook on that score.

We gave each other a detached hug and parted ways.

* * *

The month of May passed in a blur. Mostly I slept because being awake was too painful and when I was awake I downed a couple of pills to take away the edge and then went back to bed.

Eating was a whole issue in itself. Chrissy tried her best to nurture me, and if I wasn't so depressed I would have thought it comical to see her running about the kitchen in high heels and an apron looking like a 1950's housewife.

Surprisingly, the material girl had a natural talent in the kitchen. She practiced various recipes and they all seemed to look delicious, but I refused to eat. Food provided my body with the nourishment I needed to sustain life. But at that time in my life, living was the hardest thing for me to do.

As a result, I refused the food. This was followed by periods of ravenous hunger and several trips to the toilet when I vomited like a rabid dog. My body was all screwed up.

In the end, Chrissy threatened to hook me up to an IV, or even worse, call her dad if I didn't eat. So I got my diet into a healthy mode again but the emotional pain continued to rack my soul. Ray and I together was forever gone. I knew I wouldn't get a second chance.

He was back in L.A. and swiftly becoming the famous rock star he'd always dreamed of while I remained a small town girl working in a grocery store. He had erased me completely from his life. Ray's fans had more access to him than I did. I was in a world of pain. I wanted it all to stop.

And then one day it did.

I went to bed one night telling myself I had to get through this. I had to go on and live my life, even if it meant one day at a time. Even if I had to do it by focusing on just the moment.

That morning I woke up and the oxygen seemed to have returned to my lungs. I didn't feel like staying in bed anymore. I finally remembered I was a living, breathing human being and I had a future beyond my bed sheets. Miraculously, I felt different.

It's hard to explain the feeling I had because inside, I was emotionally dead. Maybe it was because I had swallowed so many pain killers they had transported my senses into a permanent numbing effect on my body.

I slowly exited my bedroom, but instead of heading down the stairs, I made a right turn and entered the back bedroom. It was the same bedroom where Nouri had stored all of Ray's belongings from his parents' house. I let out a sigh of relief when I opened the door and noticed his things were still there.

Looking at his personal belongings, I silently hoped, *Maybe he will come back after all.*

I knelt down beside one of the boxes and opened it up. It was Ray's old collection of CDs. Since everything was now stored on his media player it really wasn't necessary for him to come back to collect his priceless music.

The first one I spotted was an album by Bush. I never cared much for any of their songs, but I knew Ray loved them in high school.

Gavin Rossdale was his idol and he was the main reason Ray had gotten into music in the first place. I had always just assumed he envied the fact that Gavin married the hottest girl in showbiz. What guy wouldn't dream to do the same?

I snatched up the CD and put it into the stereo on top of the old spare dresser. Amping up the volume as loud as it could go, I opened the second box which contained some old clothing. I picked up an old Unspoken Words t-shirt. It was the very first band shirt they had designed.

What a memory.

Ray and Finn ordered a bunch of the shirts on some cheap, design-it-yourself website. They ordered twenty shirts and had Chrissy and I run the merchandise booth at the local Veteran's Hall downtown. That was the same night Chrissy and I knew the band was special. The shirts sold out before their first song had ended.

I brought the shirt to my face and inhaled it. It still smelled like Ray. Absentmindedly, I put the oversized shirt on over my disheveled top and wrapped myself in his memory, of a time when things were so much easier between us. I lay down on the soft carpet and waited for the tears to spill. But nothing followed. It was like my cheeks were a dried up riverbed.

I heard the phrase again. *Is that all you have to offer?*

Ray's final words to me burned into my mind. He was so hateful that last night and he meant everything he said. He was probably in Lilly's arms right now as I lay wrestling with my emotions.

I felt as if Gavin wrote this song specifically for Ray and me when he sang the song about treating his loved one poorly and getting his face bruised. Isn't that exactly what happened between Ray and me? Sometimes revenge can be sweet. I hope he enjoyed performing to a crowd full of people with a black eye caused by a runaway cell phone.

Amazingly, it sounded like Gavin's relationship was just as toxic as mine and Ray's.

The door swung open and I looked up to see Chrissy. She was standing above me wearing a sleeveless navy dress with a fold over collar decorated with three golden buttons. She almost looked like a sexy airplane stewardess from the fifties. The blue and orange scarf helped promote that imagery.

She strode over to the stereo and pressed the power button and glared at me.

"Sidney, while I'm ecstatic you made it out of bed this morning, you look atrocious. What in the hell are you doing?"

I wiped my eyes with the back of my hand and again was surprised to find they were dry. I attempted to sit up straight but before I could get a word out of my mouth. Chrissy lit into me.

"I'm not going to allow you to wallow in self-pity over that asshole. How can you still be wrapped up in him? Look at your forehead, Sidney. If Dave wasn't there to protect you, there's no telling what he would have done. Good riddance that he's finally gone."

Thankfully my stitches were the dissolvable kind and didn't require a follow-up doctor's visit because there was no way I could have gone out in public. I hadn't been anywhere in over a month. Luckily Chrissy talked her dad into writing a doctor's note which excused me from work but it didn't excuse my abrupt departure from Adrian's life.

I hadn't seen him since the night we watched *The Great Gatsby* together. I felt terrible for disappearing out of his life like that. I wondered if he was still around or if he was now back home in New Jersey.

I didn't bother arguing with Chrissy. In my heart of hearts I knew she was right. I forced myself off the floor and told her I was going to take a shower. Then I asked if she thought Bob would let me go back to work today. She agreed it was the best idea I'd had all month and then she headed downstairs to check on Granny.

I went into my room to make the phone call to Bob. He was ecstatic. Apparently, he was going through the whole, "three's a crowd in a line," thing and asked if I could come in within the next thirty minutes. Hanging up the phone, I began to shuffle through the closet in search of my work uniform.

That's when I saw Ray's failed attempt to salvage our relationship and I couldn't seem to tear my eyes from it. My beautiful dress was stuffed in the back of the closest, crumbled and dingy, reminding me of my own feelings at that moment.

Before exiting the room, I grabbed my laptop. Some things may have been better left alone but it just wasn't in my nature to live in blissful ignorance. I typed Ray's name in the search bar.

My suspicions were correct as I read the update on him. Ray had done just as he'd promised. Rene had posted his bail and put him on the next available flight back to L.A. but not before the media had gotten hold of the story.

I sat at my computer reading the story from the *Alternative Post* website. There were two separate pictures side by side: The first one being Ray's mug shot, black eye and all. The second photo was of myself, sitting in the back of the ambulance as a trail of blood flowed down my head. The headline almost made the whole thing worse, if that was even possible.

Lead vocalist of the band Unspoken Words wasn't so unspoken last night.

When push comes to shove you don't want to be anywhere near lead vocalist Ray Ryker. Longtime girlfriend Sidney Sinclair learned that the hard way after the rock star was charged with drunk and disorderly and domestic abuse charges. Watch out ladies, he may be single now, but is he really the gentleman we all dreamed of?

I slammed the laptop shut and laid my head across the desk. No wonder Ray blocked me from his life. I almost ruined his career. Ray was never going to forgive me for this.

I had one thought.

We were over.

Chapter Thirteen

Who Are You Anyway?

I played the role that was expected of me and although it was a fabrication at first, eventually it came to be the truth, and my new life began to take shape. I was no longer that helpless girl too infatuated with her first love to grow a backbone and stand up for herself. That introverted sheepish girl was gone, and in her place, stood an imitation of what I once was.

I was now just a fraud.

Detective Albright would periodically give me updates on the case but nothing ever broke.

"I just need one interview with Mr. Ryker, but those lawyers of his are out of this world. He has an entire staff of high powered attorneys that continue to put up road blocks. It's amazing what a little bit of money and power can do for someone."

I guess Ray was inaccessible to more than just me.

I sat in the detective's dark, dreary office as he briefed me on his investigation. It had been a week since I had entered back into this world as a productive citizen and I had decided to stop by the police station on my way to work and see what leads may have been established on Nouri's case. Or lack there of.

Of course going after Ray was ridiculous. Chrissy was right, it was obviously the meds talking when I had suspected him for a millisecond that day in the hospital. Ray would never have hurt me. There was only one person who could have been responsible.

"Have you gotten a chance to interview Lilly Lavelle?" I questioned the detective while gripping the Styrofoam cup of coffee.

Just mentioning her name made my entire body tense up. I patted my jean pocket and began to relax once I felt my pill bottle inside.

The detective shook his round face as he sat back in his swivel chair with a look of exasperation. "Ms. Lavelle is ten times harder to talk to than Ryker. It's as if I'm chasing a ghost. I can't find any record of a Lilly Lavelle living in the entire Los Angeles County."

He tossed some papers across his desk as if it were a white flag he was throwing down in surrender. "I'm sorry, Miss Sinclair, but unless your boyfriend starts talking, it looks like we may never know who was behind the murder of your grandmother's nurse."

There was a pause while the detective struggled with how to phrase his next question. "Have you decided whether or not you would like to press charges against Mr. Ryker for the domestic assault?"

His question took me by surprise. Never once did I toy with the idea of pressing charges against Ray. I had done enough damage already just with the media coverage. Not to mention the photographs that made it ten times worse. The articles made Ray out to be a monster, as if his own hands caused the damage to my forehead. The press had no idea that I was already injured when Ray and I struggled a bit. Ray never meant to hurt me physically, there was no way.

Then a very selfish thought came to my mind. I looked up and met Detective Albright's glare full on and asked, "What if I did press charges against Ray? Would I get to see him again?"

I quickly modified my question to make it sound less desperate and more causal, "I mean, I would have to see him in court, right?"

The look of an apology washed over the detective's face and he explained that even if I did decide to press charges, the D.A. still had a chance to drop them and it was very likely they would.

"Why?" I asked, astonished. The proof was there, pictures and all. "Why would they drop the case?"

"Let's just say that *Black Millennium Records* recently donated a hefty sum of money toward the Noddington Heights Police Department. The donation will basically keep us employed for the next two years."

I couldn't believe what I was hearing. Ray's record label paid off the city's police force in order to keep him from ever seeing me again. And the police force accepted?

Even though I never thought Ray had intentionally meant to hurt me, it still angered me that my injuries didn't seem to matter.

To anybody.

The joys of living in a small town amounted to an inadequate police force that was very susceptible to bribes. I thanked the detective and left for work. It looked like I was never going to see Ray again, and even worse, whoever Nouri's killer was—they were going to get off scot free. I just hoped they didn't return for me.

Samael's coming for you, Sidney. Don't let the dreams or his charm fool you. It's all lies.

No matter what I did, I couldn't shake my mother's warning. What if my dream wasn't a dream at all, but more a premonition? Then than means Samael is already here. That I have already met him . . .

Adrian showed up around the same time my dreams began, could it be more than coincidence that he holds the same alluring green eyes as the man in my dreams? I pushed the disturbing thought from my mind. No way. If he was, then that would mean he was responsible for my injuries and that was something I would never believe.

* * *

At work, I brushed my hand against the black rubber belt causing the products to slowly come down the line. One by one I began scanning the items: Diet soda, bananas, four pre-made ham and cheese sandwiches . . .

My eyes shot up.

I almost jumped out of my skin when I saw that black hair falling in front of those unmistakable green eyes.

"Adrian." I gasped. My mind was racing as I quickly attempted to reassemble my thoughts. "Uh, how have you been?"

He handed me a twenty-dollar bill and I quickly stuffed it into the register and began counting out his change.

"Confused," he answered. "You sort of disappeared on me."

I handed him his change and glanced inside the paper bag and rolled my eyes.

"Seriously? Are you incapable of eating anything substantial other than sandwiches?" I joked, intentionally ignoring his last statement.

He shrugged and grabbed the bag. "I'm not much of a cook. See you around."

Before I could gather my thoughts, my inner self unleashed itself and the pent-up words escaped my lips before I had a chance to modify them. "I get off work in twenty minutes. Will you be around?"

Holding my breath in anticipation I could feel my cheeks turning vulnerable red.

"Sure," he said, as that familiar smile returned to his lips. "I'll meet you outside."

* * *

All I could see was his silhouette and the red glow from his cigarette. We had been walking for a couple of miles and decided to stop and rest at the cemetery. He brought the cigarette to his lips and took a long drag.

After letting out a cloud of smoke he asked, "What if life was nothing more than a dream?"

I sat in the dark for a long time while I pondered his question. I'd often had the same thought about life. I've thought about it even more since I met him. How else could it explain how I had initially dreamt this man up, and then he had appeared as someone very real to me? I mean not exactly, my dream guy and he had different names, but Samael did harbor some strong similarities to Adrian.

"I suppose it could be," I answered.

"My words can change your life, Sidney, if you'd only start to believe them."

Another pause while he inhaled his toxicity. "They can also destroy you, if you let them."

I rolled my eyes as I embraced myself for more of his riddles.

Even in the dark, Adrian noticed my lack of interest. "Don't look away like you don't care to listen to what I have to say."

He had some anger in his voice. He appeared to be in one of his moods again. There was more behind his words and it bothered me that he couldn't just say the words he wanted to.

"Is this world really where you want live?" he asked.

I snorted and then kicked the rocks next to my feet, "As if I really have a choice."

Ignoring my sarcasm, Adrian continued with his nonsense, "I read a story once, it was a long time ago and of course I don't remember all of the details, but I do remember the point of the story. There was this woman, and her life seemed to be falling apart."

Sounds familiar.

"Throughout the story, she was being haunted by some entity. I can't remember how exactly, maybe through dreams or some kind of medium."

Sounds very familiar.

"Anyway, long story short . . ." He smirked and looked over at me. "Mainly because I don't remember it. The girl woke up, and when she did she was in the place of her dreams. That person haunting her was her real self. She lived a life of eternity and every time she fell asleep she would dream up this entire fictional life. What if that's really what happens? What if no one really dies here but instead they just wake up?"

He took another drag of his cigarette and then flicked it onto someone's plot. We both watched the red glow fade into nothing. Adrian hopped off a little statue platform and slowly started to walk toward me.

He sat down and looked into my eyes, searching for something. Understanding, perhaps.

"That sounds too good to be true," I whispered.

It was a great story, and for a microsecond, I was amazed at how much I related to it, but to just be able to wake up and have all of this crap be a dream? I'd woken up every morning for the past month wishing this was one big dream but it's not. I'm still stuck in this town with my sick grandmother and Ray still hates me. This story didn't relate to me at all.

But it did make me want my pills.

Pulling the bottle out of my purse, I tossed two pills into my mouth.

Adrian narrowed his eyes, "You're the one who said so yourself that day in my car; that perhaps life is just some kind of illusion. That we leave when conditions are no longer sufficient."

I brought my knees up to my chest and wrapped my arms around them. It was getting cold out here. "If life was a dream, I would have been able to force myself awake and out of this nightmare already."

Adrian sat back and pulled out his pack of Marlboros. He shook the pack and snatched a cigarette with his mouth. He was about to light it when I grabbed it.

"I hate it when you smoke," I pleaded.

Adrian turned his head and frowned at me. He put the cigarette back in the pack and put them in the pocket of his jeans, then took my hand in his.

I loved being with him, even when he got all worked up with his crazy talk. It felt good just to sit here with him, in the dark, lost in our thoughts, holding hands . . .

He pressed his nose against my hair and inhaled deeply, "Where did you go?"

The question overwhelmed me with a deep sadness. I took a breath and let out a long wistful sigh. Adrian squeezed my hand and intertwined his fingers with mine as he looked at me.

I answered him truthfully, "Crazy, I guess."

He let go of my hand and ran both hands through his shiny black hair. Looking up at the stars he answered, "But you're back now."

I let myself breathe again. "Yes, I'm back now."

He took my hand in his again, "That's good, because I really missed you."

I gave myself a pep talk, *Come on, Sidney. You can do this. Tell him how you feel.*

Adrian looked over at me, waiting for me to say something.

Avoiding all eye contact, I replied, "I really enjoy spending time with you."

And I think maybe I'm falling in love with you.

Adrian smiled and gave my hand a tug, pulling my body closer. His body heat wrapped around me like a blanket. "I like spending time with you too, Sidney. That's why I'm here."

"I know."

I had so much more to tell him, but I couldn't force the words out of my mouth.

I also couldn't end the night without knowing the answer to the question that burned in my mind.

"Are you still in love with your old girlfriend?" I asked, this time I forced my eyes to stay on his. He smiled his crooked smile and gave me a slight nod of his head.

"I'll always love her," he answered. "Now come on, we better get you back home. Besides, I need a cigarette."

He laughed as he nudged me with his arm.

Chapter Fourteen

Getting Over You

Everyone wants a good story. They don't care if you hurt, if you cry, or if you bleed. As long as it's good, they'll be by your side cheering you on. I guess that's what happened with Ray and me, because nobody gave a crap about my boyfriend's band until I met Adrian. After that night at the cemetery, my life—scratch that—*our* lives had changed forever.

The month of September was now coming to an end and I still hadn't spoken to Ray, but another one of his songs was being played on the radio and their debut album had been released.

I guess after his arrest, he had gone back to L.A. and put all of his concentration into that album. He recorded the final three songs and amended the one the label had not agreed with.

His music had changed. What used to be soft harmonious love songs played with drums and the electric guitars had now been transformed into a darker style fusion of dissonance and cacophony. The word love was replaced with hate and vocal screams echoed about revenge before dropping back into the melancholy chorus.

The fans ate it up and demanded more as they hung onto every word Ray sang.

I hung onto just one word.

At first the word was hate, but slowly it changed.

Because it was never a definitive hate. He would sing lines like, "*Maybe I should hate you.*"

If ever there was a time to hang onto a word, the time was now and the word was maybe.

The word held so many possibilities. Like *maybe* he doesn't hate me. *Maybe* he would still forgive me. But if that was the case then why did he block my number? Why hadn't he tried to call me?

Needless to say, every fan added to Ray's list became my nemesis. They hated the person who could bring such a man as Ray Ryker into disparity. They never stopped to consider the fact that every story had *two* sides. I was voiceless in that world. This was his universe now. He was the dictator.

The band's new single had a video *MTV* would play late at night and I'd be a liar had I claimed ignorance about it. Of course, I had watched it. The song was too beautiful not to enjoy.

It was one of the few love songs he'd left on his album. He was playing the piano and revealed to me that he still had a soul with actual feelings. This made me angry because, once again, he got to play the part of a sad, broken-hearted guy that had been ruined by his mean-spirited girlfriend.

All his fans were lining up to send sympathy to such a vulnerable guy who was not afraid to show his feelings. I saw right through him and I knew his act was complete bullshit.

Although Rene must have been happy with the whole outcome, I bet she never dreamt in a million years our relationship would help ignite her boy to the brink of stardom, in turn, generating millions of dollars for the label. I wondered how big her end-of-the-year bonus would be this Christmas.

The first week the single came out, I downloaded it and played it relentlessly trying to decipher its true meaning the same way I used to despise his fans for doing so. I concluded the song was about us. He spoke about letting someone go but not giving up on the love they shared. And the most heart-wrenching lyric was when he sang *"I won't kiss you goodbye."*

It flooded my brain with that terrible memory in front of the bar when his hands were shackled behind his back as Detective Albright patiently waited to haul him off to jail.

I had attempted to kiss him and he turned his face away from me. At the time he did it in anger, but in the song, he sings about denying the kiss because he was simply refusing to allow his lover to leave him.

How convenient, Ray.

Really?

Because if that's what he meant, then why hadn't he tried to call me? It had been six months since that fateful night and in the blink of an eye, Ray and I went from being epic lovers to saddened strangers.

I got out of bed and forced myself to prepare for the day. I put on my denim skinny jeans with a gray shirt and tan boots. Plugging in my hair wand, I began to curl the ends of my hair.

This had been a new look for me that Chrissy had helped me achieve shortly after I snapped out of my depression. She was right to suggest shedding my old image and replacing it with another after a trauma had changed my life.

After applying my makeup, I checked myself over in the mirror and then grabbed my purse and keys as I headed toward the front door.

Then I saw Chrissy on the couch with my favorite ice cream and the thought of lolling around the house with her seemed to be just what my body and mind needed.

"Hey," she said, with a mouth full of frozen mint chocolate chip.

I nodded in response and took a seat next to her. "What's up?"

Chrissy waxed philosophical as she stared blankly at the television screen. "Do you ever regret breaking up with Ray?"

Now it was my turn to stare blankly at the T.V.

It hurt me deeply the way Ray and I had ended things. But what hurt most was how quickly we had grown into strangers. He was like a piece of coral that had broken away from the Great Barrier Reef. He floated off into the sea while all the rest of us little people were trapped on the island.

Unspoken Words had released their debut album and it launched them into instant fame. These months apart, Ray had not only toured the country, he toured the world. The band was nominated for a ton of awards and they actually won in the category of "Breakthrough Band of the Year."

Every one of his dreams had come true and with it, I had grown into a distant memory, a childhood romance he simply outgrew as he transitioned into adulthood.

Maybe if I was lucky enough, his social media coordinator could unblock me, but that was about as close I could ever get to Ray Ryker, the rock star, for now.

Chrissy and I had settled into a nice routine which involved hours of television and gallons of ice cream. I think by watching the band's success, Chrissy was finally starting to have some regret of ending things with Finn. Ignoring her question, I tried to focus on something that would easily catch her full attention.

Herself.

I adeptly played to her narcissism, "So how was your date last night?"

"It was great, until he lifted his hat and there was a head full of *gray* hair!" she exclaimed.

We both broke into laughter.

She had been set up on a date with the guy by one of the nurses she had gone to school with. The man was a highly paid doctor, so of course Chrissy jumped at the opportunity. Sight unseen, Chrissy arrived at the restaurant and was impressed by his appearance until . . . he sat down at the table and removed his hat. To say she agonized all the way through her dinner would be an understatement.

He was in his early thirties and while he looked handsome enough, Chrissy was much too vain to date a man who was graying prematurely.

"So you weren't into the silver fox look then?" I joked with her as I scooped out another spoonful of ice cream.

"No way, I'd much rather have a dark panther." She meowed and clawed the air looking like a cat in heat.

"I think you already had one of those."

She absorbed my comment about Finn and shot back, "Yeah, and let's not forget your golden goddess."

"Oh geez, enough already, this is so pathetic."

We both agreed and continued stuffing our faces in silence. Finally, Chrissy grabbed the remote control and began to stream the latest music awards show. There was no way I was ready to sit there and watch as Ray soaked in compliments and sympathy from all sorts of strangers. I needed to emotionally remove myself from what was about to take place.

Although Chrissy and I seemed to be gaining some good days, there was only one person who could stop my ever-growing pain. Adrian couldn't heal the wound completely, but he could apply pressure, which would temporarily slow the bleeding from my heart and instead allow it to gradually slow down to a trickle.

I stood up and stretched my arms.

"I'm going to go on a walk," I announced as I reached into my jeans pocket and took out my prescription bottle of pills. Adrian could only immobilize my bleeding heart. The painkillers were still very much needed to do the rest.

Chrissy rolled her eyes to let me know she wasn't so easily fooled, "You mean you're going to get a side of Adrian with those pills you've been eating like candy?"

Thankfully she had talked her father into extending the prescription for me. I shrugged as I headed toward the front door. "I won't be gone too long. See you in a bit."

"He must not be that good in bed if he still has you pining over your ex," she shouted in defiance.

I had told Chrissy time and time again that Adrian and I were just friends but she never bought it. She didn't grasp the idea that a male and a female could be friends without having sex. I didn't have the energy to argue about it and so I just let her believe what she wanted.

Adrian and I had grown closer over the last few months, although I had finally admitted to myself that I had stronger feelings for him, I still had not managed to vocally admit that to his face. Or Chrissy's for that matter.

* * *

It's hard to explain exactly how I had fallen in love with him. Maybe it was the fact that he never hid his emotions behind that beautiful face of his.

Those penetrating orbs were never afraid to look away. Instead, they probed, questioned, and exhilarated my soul, always determined to uncover my dark sad thoughts and always there to catch me when I fell.

It became a habit for Adrian to come over every Saturday and together we walked the three mile trek that I used to run. I missed running, but the new Sidney had been slowed to a walk. The running Sidney had died the night at the bar. The new Sidney would stand and face her challenges head on because running, no matter how fast or how far, always proved to get me nowhere.

I enjoyed the company with Adrian rather than the company in my head that cruelly told me what a terrible mistake I'd made losing Ray.

This morning we were about to turn around and head back home when I noticed him glancing up at the old rusty train trestle above our heads.

"Pretty ugly, huh?" I asked, nodding at the bridge. "The city put up a fight to have the train company repaint it but since then, they've been arguing back and forth with each other, unable to decide whose job it was to paint it."

"It's obvious, isn't it?" Adrian answered. "I'd say since it's the train company's property, it would be their responsibility." He continued to stare at the bridge. "Have you ever been up there?"

That stretch of railroad was the exact spot where my mother had stepped out in front of a moving train almost twenty years before.

"Yeah, there's a hiking trail on the other side of the freeway over-pass, then there's a staircase that leads you to a tunnel the train goes through," I explained without mentioning my personal history associ-ated with the area.

He looked over at me. "Really?"

"Do you want to check it out?"

I had been coming to this place every day during my runs, but I had always gone alone. Now I had suddenly put myself in a position to share the most sacred place in my life. I wasn't sure if I could do it.

Adrian was sure. "Fuck yeah."

And so we began climbing up the trestle. It took us about fifteen minutes to get up to the tunnel. I sat on the wooden stairs while Adrian walked around exploring.

Stretching my legs, I clutched my gray hoodie tighter. Adrian came back over and sat down next to me on the staircase.

I smiled weakly. "So is it all you imagined it to be?"

He nodded and bumped me with his arm. "Of course it was."

I rested my head on his shoulder and closed my eyes. The warmth of his body engulfed me like it often did. I turned to look into those green eyes, and before I could stop myself, the words fumbled out of my mouth, "Why did you have to come here and meet me now?"

I could see the look on Adrian's face as he tried to piece together the meaning of my question. Instead of answering he pulled his cigarettes out of his pocket.

Great, now I've frustrated him.

"I just wish we could have met at a different time, when my mind wasn't so messed up."

He lit his cigarette and enjoyed the first few drags before responding, "Maybe we were supposed to meet while you were so messed up."

I raised my eyebrow in speculation of his theory.

He smiled. "I know you think that soul mates are found based on a person's musical preferences, but what if soul mates are brought together to fix each other?"

I didn't know how to answer other than to reply with a joke. "I suppose I had better go search for a heart surgeon then."

My necklace slipped out from inside my sweatshirt and was dangling in midair. It caught Adrian's attention and he reached over and picked up the pendant, examining it closer. I watched his face as he did it. It was almost as if a dark shadow was cast over him as I witnessed the pain he so desperately tried to hide from me resurface in his eyes. I couldn't bear having him handle it, so I took the pendant and tucked it back inside my sweatshirt.

"You still miss her." I said it softly, trying to be sensitive.

If he could listen to all of my heartache, it was only fair I allowed him the same opportunity. He bit his lower lip, using his teeth to force his mouth shut, but the sadness in his eyes told me everything. Instead of responding, he stood up and walked a few steps away, and took another drag of his cigarette.

I walked over and stood in front of him, inches from his face. His green eyes looked at me in question with a cigarette dangling loosely from his mouth. I reached up and removed the cigarette, never taking my eyes off him. We stood facing each other, playing a game of chicken, waiting for the other to make the first move. Finally, he took my hand in an attempt to take the cigarette back. I tightened my grip, careful not to burn myself as my eyes never left his.

"Why don't you ever try to kiss me?"

As soon as I said it I wished I could take it back.

Adrian became still as a statue, his eyes unreadable. I wanted to run away and crawl under a rock, but the question had been burning in my mind for so long I had to know. We had spent so much time together these last months and aside from the night at the bar, he had never put a move on me. He had to feel the same connection I felt. I tried to ignore it because of Ray but what was his reason?

"Because you still haven't figured it out," he said coldly, removing the cigarette from my fingers and placing it back in his mouth.

I stood there, confused by his answer.

"I don't understand. Maybe you can just tell me what I'm supposed to figure out."

"*Maybe* isn't good enough, Sidney. People need to be sure, and if you can't figure that out on your own, then I can't help you. It's getting late and I have to get back home. We should have never come up here," he said angrily.

I slowly followed him down the trail, the numbness setting into my body, acting as a shield to protect my frazzled nerves.

We walked the entire way home in silence. He was too angry to speak and I was too scared to provoke him. When we got to the bottom of my steps, I turned to go inside when I felt a tug on the back of my sweatshirt.

I turned around and he pulled me into a hug. "I'm sorry, Sidney. I had a great time today. Thank you for taking me up there. I'll see you later, 'k?"

"I lied to you that day in the cemetery," I blurted out.

Once again my mouth failed to wait for my mind to catch up to decide if the words I wanted to spill out had been emotionally approved.

Adrian tightened his grip around me as his expression darkened. "Lied to me how?"

"I told you I didn't have any relatives buried there. It was a lie. My mother's buried in that cemetery so I wasn't trespassing that day."

Adrian seemed relieved that my lie was a small one. He pulled me closer to him and embraced me in a soothing manner.

"Don't worry about it, Sidney. We have the rest of our lives to learn everything about each other."

"She died on that train trestle when I was a baby. She committed suicide by jumping in front of a train."

I didn't know why I had felt the need to share this bit of information with Adrian, but I did know that it felt good to get it off of my chest.

Adrian gently took my hand and led me to the stairs to take a seat. He wanted to talk now.

Chapter Fifteen

Flicker, fade

Today, once again, Adrian proved to be my safety net as I continued my free fall into the abyss of sadness while explaining the absence of my mother. We were both perched on the front steps of Granny's Craftsman. Adrian graciously provided his open ear.

Just then the postman walked up, carrying a large box, "Sidney Sinclair?"

I nodded and signed for the package. Adrian watched intently as the courier placed the parcel in my hands and headed back down the stairs.

"I swear this better not be another thing from Ray's house," I complained while examining the box.

Even though I wasn't on speaking terms with Ray's family since they had expelled me from their presence, they continued to find it perfectly acceptable to mail his old belongings to me, as though I was his off-site storage facility.

Or maybe they were expecting we'd get back together eventually.

Maybe being the operative word here.

"I can send him a legal letter for removal of personal property if you want." Adrian offered.

He was just trying to be helpful but we both knew I would never send Ray legal threats.

Especially not from Adrian McAlister.

"I'm serious," he said as he sat two steps below me.

This time he did not turn around to face me as he spoke. I stared at the back of his head waiting for him to continue. Instead, he reached into the front pocket of his denim jeans and began pulling out his damn Marlboro Reds.

"Is that a new shirt?" I asked, attempting to change the subject.

He turned around and looked up at me with the cigarette hanging on his bottom lip. He was wearing an olive green garage shirt. I'd never seen him in that color before. In fact, most of the time he stuck to the depressing color of black. Thinking of the color black reminded me of yet another question.

"Hey, do you dye your hair?"

It was midnight black with no hint of any other color even as it reflected off the sun. And the color against his pale face made it look washed out and unnatural.

He snatched the unlit cigarette out of his mouth and climbed up the steps to sit next to me. My heart began to pound as it always did when he got too close and invaded my personal space.

He leaned over and whispered in my ear. "You notice a lot of things about me, Sidney." He dragged his lips over my lobe and breathed. "Why?"

Because you're all I ever think about.

I sat as still as a statue looking straight ahead, too nervous to look at him. He didn't move his face and I could feel his hot breath on my ear. I gripped the wooden stair next to me with both hands and closed my eyes, waiting for him to go back down to his step.

"Don't let him come back this time. You deserve better."

I felt a gush of cold wind as he jumped up and galloped down the stairs. I opened my eyes and thought about pursuing him but stopped myself. He was on the sidewalk lighting his cigarette.

"Wait," I yelled out.

He looked up at me. Those pendant eyes full of hope, as if he was waiting for certain words to fall from my lips.

But I hadn't a clue what words he wanted to hear. What words would make him stay?

"You didn't answer my questions," I stalled, trying to buy time.

He took a long drag of the cigarette and exhaled a gray cloud of toxins and began walking, "You didn't answer mine either," he shouted over his shoulder.

I turned around and marched into the house with the mysterious package in my hands.

Chapter Sixteen

Resurface

Chrissy was seated exactly where I had left her. The empty container of ice cream was now on the coffee table and Chrissy's eyes were glued to the screen. The awards show was still on as the familiar song was playing on the television set.

There he was, a miniature Ray on the tube, wearing a white suit with a black tie playing on a matching baby grand piano. He was singing the song the world was gobbling up at a record pace.

The cameras focused on him as he played and sang with so much emotion as the words passionately exploded from his lips, "I won't kiss you goodbye."

After the first few minutes of the song, the black curtain behind him dropped and the remaining band members appeared and began to play. I stood frozen in place, clutching the package as I glanced over at Chrissy.

Finn was now playing a guitar solo and she sat on the couch clutching an accent pillow with the same emotional fierceness I was feeling. I couldn't take anymore and I finally forced myself to grab the remote and turn the television set off.

Immediately Chrissy withdrew from her trance and looked up at me., "Hey, Sidney. How was your walk?"

"Good. How's Granny?"

"She's well. I just finished giving her a sponge bath."

I smiled in gratitude and sat down on the couch next to my best friend. She grabbed her cell phone and began pressing some buttons. I guess she hadn't gotten her fill of torture because now, she began watching a video interview on her cell phone with Unspoken Words via YouTube. Ignoring the video, I went across the room and began fumbling with the package the postman had delivered. I had to find a better way to occupy my time.

I could still hear Chrissy's phone and even though I was trying to block out the voices, I could hear everything.

A reporter was asking Ray about the meaning of the songs on the album. They wanted to confirm if the rumors were true about the songs being about his ex-girlfriend back home in Northern California.

"Did he have any contact with her since his arrest…blah, blah, blah."

I pretended to be opening the box but now I was straining my ears to listen to Ray's response.

"No, I haven't had any contact with Sid since that night. It's actually been one of the hardest things I've ever had to do. But staying away from her is best, because honestly she deserves better."

Bullshit, I thought, *You stay away because you hate me. You'll never forgive me for that night.*

He continued to stab me with emotional daggers. "The majority of the songs written do stem from our past relationship."

There was a long pause before he continued, "With the exception of one."

As soon as he said that, I knew the song he was referring to. There was a song on the album that I couldn't relate to and I didn't understand the lyrics Ray was singing about. He was referring to someone else.

The song pointed to a mystery woman claiming she had held him down and made him live in a false world she created for him. It went on to express it had come time for him to break away and find himself on his own because he doesn't need to be molded into what she had wanted.

The rest of the interview was interrupted with Chrissy's loud shriek as she dropped her phone and stared at me in horror.

"What?" I asked, dying to know who that song was written for.

"That creep has gone too far this time!" Chrissy yelled as she reached down and scooped her phone off the floor.

Before I could respond, her ear was pressed against her pink-jeweled phone and it was ringing. I sat back, ready to watch the show, wondering if I should make some popcorn. My mouth flew open when I heard the familiar voice on the other end answer her call.

"Your cousin has pushed me too far this time, Finn. He had no right to write a song about you and me!"

I stood there gaping with a look of total shock on my face. It was as if I was seated to watch a PG film and an adult movie began to play. I was so flabbergasted by the events unfolding that I just stood there, staring at Chrissy in disbelief.

First, I couldn't believe she was actually on the phone with Finn, and second, I really couldn't believe that the song Ray wrote was about Finn and Chrissy. It was even more incomprehensible that Ray would let the entire world know how he felt about Chrissy breaking his cousin's heart.

I heard Finn as he chuckled on the other end of the line. "Babe, if I knew that Ray writing a song about us would get you to call me, I would have had Ray write a whole album about you."

Chrissy's face turned a bright shade of pink as Finn still referred to her as babe. He said it so casually, as if no time apart could change that.

"I don't want Ray putting my business out there. You got that Finn Aldman? Otherwise, I'm going to fly down to L.A. and kick his pansy ass!"

More chuckles from Finn. "Why go all the way to L.A.? You can do it tonight in San Francisco. By the way, Ray wanted to know if Sidney got his package."

As soon as he said it, I dropped the box like a hand grenade and jumped back, afraid it might blow me up.

I met Chrissy's eyes, shrugged my shoulders, and mumbled to her, "I had no idea that package was from Ray."

She cut off her sort of boyfriend, "I have to go. Goodbye, Finn."

He subtly pleaded with her, "Maybe I'll see you tonight, huh?"

"Doubtful."

She tossed the phone on the couch, held her hands in the air, and jumped up and down, squealing as if she'd just won the lottery.

"He still called me babe. He still loves me, I know he does!"

Chrissy made no sense at all. She had spent the entire year sure that she didn't want to be with Finn. But then, she constantly complained she was miserable without him, and now when she's presented with a second chance, she gave him the cold shoulder.

And she's happy about it?

He had asked to see her. He practically begged her on the phone and she responded with a negative. Chrissy was now playing hard to get. Was she crazy?

She ran across the living room and snatched up the package. "What are you waiting for, Sidney? Open it."

I tried my best to steady my shaking hands as I began to open the big brown box, but they wouldn't stop trembling.

Finally, impatience got the better of Chrissy and she pushed me aside and began tearing into the box as if she were a child ravaging her Christmas presents.

Inside there was a gorgeous navy blue cocktail dress. I lifted it up to examine it more closely. It was a simple short-sleeved number that looked to be knee length. It would have been ordinary if not for the thousands of sequins stitched to the dress, making it as heavy as a sack of potatoes. This dress screamed dollar bills and I knew there was only one person that could have sent it. My hand shook as I reached in the box, searching for a note. At the bottom of the box lay a pale blue envelope. I picked it up with my still shaking hands and removed the card from the envelope.

The front side read, "*I miss being us.*"

I opened it up and immediately recognized Ray's handwriting.

> *The memory of that night haunts me. I lied when I said I was never holding on. The truth is I've been holding on for dear life ever since I met you. I'll never let you go. Meet me tonight for dinner. The address is below. I'll be waiting. If you don't come, I will understand. I know I messed up big time. Ray.*

The address was in San Francisco. Finn must have known that Ray was going to ask me to meet him tonight. And he had asked Chrissy to come along. I stared into Chrissy's big hazel eyes, silently asking her to give me some sort of guidance. She didn't let me down.

"You have to go."

I countered, "I'll only go if you come with me. Either we both go or neither one of us goes."

As I said this, I had to push Adrian's face out of my head. Moments before he was breathing in my ear not to give Ray another chance and now I was considering the exact thing he had warned me against.

I began to get angry because I had boldly asked Adrian to kiss me and he had turned me away without a second thought. Maybe if Adrian had kissed me, I wouldn't be considering meeting Ray tonight. In my mind, Adrian had his chance and he blew it. He was always speaking in those silly riddles and telling me that I hadn't figured them out. As if my love was somehow shallow and dispassionate. I was done playing mind games.

I was headed for San Francisco.

Chapter Seventeen

Fall for You

Maybe it was stupid of me to go. I'm almost positive it was, but that's me; always going against my better judgment when it came to Ray. He and I constantly entangled ourselves into a disastrous web of chaos, and we liked to fool ourselves into thinking it was a relationship. Sadly, I always ended up being the fly while he reigned supreme as the spider.

It had been six months since that night in front of the bar, and although I ended up losing the love of my life, I had gained my own identity. For the first time in two years, I was finding myself, I was finding happiness again.

This past summer, I had found my voice and in it I had also found my freedom. Was I ready to throw that all away and crawl back into my prison with Ray, into my own personal cell of loneliness and desperation?

Maybe it will be different this time, I foolishly reasoned with myself.

I took a deep breath and started fanning my perfectly made-up face. I could feel myself hyperventilating as I stood in the lobby of The Fairmont Hotel.

My bff noticed. "Calm down, Sidney, you look fab. I made sure of that."

Chrissy squeezed my hand as she whispered the words of encouragement to me. It didn't take much to convince her to come tonight. She had strongly maintained that the only reason she was taking this trip was to give Finn a piece of her mind, and insist that he never speak of their personal history again.

But I was Chrissy's closest confidant and I knew that deep down, she loved every second of this drama. Being in the emotional spotlight is what this girl craved. She always had to be the center of attention in high school and now she was staring into the possibility of being the center of the universe.

"Where are you meeting Finn?"

She nodded to the left. "There's a café around the corner. I told him to meet me there. I'm not trying to get all intimate like you and Ray."

Chrissy said this while she eyed the entrance to the restaurant Ray had specified as our agreed upon destination. It was very intimate and at the same time, intimidating. I began to fan myself more aggressively now. Why was it so damn hot in here?

Chrissy tilted her head, giving me a look of dismay. "Calm down, Sidney. You look like you're about to walk into your own firing squad. It's just dinner and it's just Ray."

Her pep talk worked and I took a deep breath and gave Chrissy a hug. We said our goodbyes and we both turned in opposite directions and headed to face our men.

But as soon as Chrissy disappeared all of my self-doubt returned and I repressed the urge to run.

That was the old Sidney. The new Sidney doesn't run away.

I took another deep breath and entered the restaurant. The place was packed and I knew I could easily turn around and escape through the lobby doors before anyone ever noticed me. But I pushed myself forward and approached the greeter at the wooden pedestal. She was a petite blonde girl with wire rimmed glasses.

"Good evening, Miss. Do you have a reservation tonight?"

"I do. I believe it's under Ray Ryker."

As soon as I said his name, the blonde's eyes shot up at me and gave me a once over as she sized me up. I silently prayed she didn't recognize me from the tabloids. His fans hated me for supposedly breaking his heart.

She grabbed her yellow highlighter and searched the long list of names on the white sheet of paper in front of her.

"Ah, here we go. He reserved the best seat in the house for you. It must be a special occasion, hmm?" she said icily.

I smiled and reddened a bit but kept my lips shut. I wasn't about to give anything away.

She grabbed two menus and turned toward the dining room. "Follow me, please."

We walked past a large indoor fountain and weaved through the white pillars that gave the place a "Caesars Palace" sort of look. The dining room was decorated in shades of gold, white, and tan and in the center of the room was a giant dome ceiling with a massive crystal chandelier.

We crossed the dining floor and entered a smaller, quieter room. There was an older man wearing a black tuxedo tucked away in the corner playing softly on the piano. I spotted Ray and immediately all of those old feelings resurfaced. He stood up upon my arrival.

"You came," he breathed, a sigh of relief escaping his lips. He stared only at me and I wondered if he even noticed the hostess that had brought me to him, even though her eyes followed Ray like a hawk, desperately trying to get him to notice her.

He looked perfect, as always. His blond hair was combed back, revealing his high forehead and big blue eyes. There was a slight darkness under his eyes which showed he hadn't been getting much sleep. He also had a bit of stubble on his chin.

With the tired look, he looked older, more mature, and wiser. It was as if I was now staring at the adult version of Ray, no longer that self-centered kid I knew six months ago.

I sat down at the chair across from him and he went back to his seat. The hostess went over the list of specials, talking only to Ray, and handed him our menus. He ignored the entrees and grabbed my hand, never allowing his eyes to leave mine. He told her to bring us a bottle of their most expensive wine. Of course she didn't card him as she went off in pursuit of the vino; he was freakin' Ray Ryker, for god's sake.

He gave me a warm smile, "How are you? You look great, Sid, your hair's different."

How am I? I chomp prescription pills like they're candy out of a Pez dispenser. All so that I can remain numb to the fact that you dropped me like a bad habit.

I gave him a sparkling, forced smile.

I nervously twirled my long brown curls in my hand and responded, "The benefit of having Chrissy as a roommate, I suppose."

Taking a sip of the water that was already on the table, I added, "Thank you for the dress."

He gripped my hand tighter.

Was he still allowed to do that?

I thought that right was revoked the night he left me on my own, banged, battered, and broken in front of the bar. He became a stranger to me that night, and had continued in that manner over the last six months. Ray must have seen the dismay on my face because his grip loosened and he withdrew the intrusive hand.

"I'm sorry. It's just habit, you know; touching you."

I should have let him sweat and made him realize what he'd lost. The right to touch me was no longer his. But that was my ongoing problem with him; I never could deny Ray anything. Never could say no to him, and tonight proved to be no different.

I reached across the table and gripped his hand. "No, it's fine really." Forcing a smile, I squeezed his hand as a reassurance, even though I wasn't so sure myself.

"We moved out of the mansion last week. I couldn't bring myself to leave the clothes that were meant for you. Even though you never touched them, they still reminded me of you and I couldn't let you go. So I packed them up and brought them with me."

I ignored the fact that the closet only brought back the horrid images of Lilly exiting as she was wearing *my* dress. A woman never forgets that kind of memory.

"You look good too, Ray. I like your outfit, you look a little gangster." I smiled. "Like a young Al Capone." I giggled.

He was wearing a light blue dress shirt with a navy blue vest. A gold tie poked out from under the vest. With that outfit and the slicked back hair all I could think of was, "*Boardwalk Empire.*"

We sat in silence, not quite knowing what to say to each other so instead we just stared, both unable to believe that the other was sitting so close. It was like a dream, and it was quite ridiculous. I felt like a nervous school girl on my first prom. That's how I felt in front of him now, like I was sitting on pins and needles as my stomach gurgled. I had known Ray since our freshman year of high school and we had been the best of friends. We knew each other so well we could literally have a silent conversation with just our eyes. But now, as I was sitting across from him in this lavish San Francisco restaurant, wearing this costly blue dress, I couldn't even muster up the courage to ask him to pass the salt.

I could feel the heat on my flushed face as I nervously tapped the side of my water glass, not quite sure where to place my hands, just knowing I had to keep them busy. I snuck a glance over at him and found that he was staring at me with those intense blue eyes. I shot my eyes back down to the white linen tablecloth.

"What's the matter, Sid?"

I stumbled for the right words before I just spit them out. "You make me nervous."

Ray tilted his head to the side, looking slightly astonished. "Me?"

"Isn't that crazy? I mean we've been together forever, but then again it seems like forever ago when I knew you."

My analysis made me sad. As if by saying it out loud, it made it true. It confirmed the fact that we had become strangers in such a short time.

"It seems like these days I only know you through your music, which kind of makes me more your fan than anything else, and now I'm sitting across a candlelight dinner in some fancy restaurant with some rock star. Yeah it makes me nervous," I concluded.

Ray sat back in the chair with his arms folded, staring at me in disbelief before bursting into uncontrollable laughter. "You can't be serious, Sid."

The pesky hostess returned, no longer wearing her eyeglasses, as if this new look would somehow grasp Ray's attention. She carried with her a bottle of red wine and a basket of bread. She uncorked it, poured some into the glasses, and let Ray know that our server would be over momentarily.

Six months ago, I would have become a jealous maniac, demanding Ray somehow fix the situation. But now, I only felt sorry for the little blonde girl who was making a complete fool of herself.

I didn't know if the change in me came from all the growing up I had done, or from the confidence I felt from the way Ray was staring at me. He looked at me as if I were the only girl in the room. Of course there was no reason to be jealous. I held 100 % of his attention.

Time spent apart did not alter my feelings for him. If anything, it intensified them. He looked so much better in person than I had ever imagined and the whole thing felt right. The puzzle pieces of my broken life were slowly fitting back together.

I grabbed my wine glass and quickly downed the contents. I needed something to take off this edge. Ray followed suit.

He must be just as nervous as I am. I laughed to myself.

At that point, a pretty girl with dirty blonde hair stepped up to our table. She probably was about my age and gorgeous.

"Ray Ryker?" she breathlessly asked.

Ray brought his heavenly blue eyes up to her and smiled his perfect smile as he extended his hand toward her.

"Oh my gosh," she gushed, "I can't believe that I'm meeting you right now." She squealed, ignoring the fact that she was interrupting dinner with his girlfriend, or whatever the hell I was.

She was so focused on Ray I don't think she ever saw me. Of course Ray was eating up all of the attention as he signed her napkin and listened to her babble on about her tickets for his show tomorrow night at The Warfield Theater. He promised to look for her in the crowd and they hugged before she anxiously ran back to her group of friends waiting on the other side of the restaurant.

I looked over at Ray and wanted to slap the stupid look off his face. I guess I was still that jealous person I was before. Some things never change.

"What?" he asked, trying to sound innocent and failing miserably.

"See? That's exactly what I mean. You're no longer Ray, my high school sweetheart, now you're Ray the hot musician with all sorts of pretty girls throwing themselves at you. I don't know how to compete with that."

"It was just an autograph, Sid," Ray said quietly, trying not to turn this conversation into a spectacle, adding to the fact that the girls had their cell phones out, trying to snap a picture to capture the memory of their shallow lives.

The last thing Ray needed was another publicized fight with me. I sat back in my chair, staring at his face, trying hard to read his expression, but I failed. He was Mount Rushmore. The connection we had as kids was non-existent and I was staring at nothing more than a stranger.

I pointedly asked him, "What would you have done if I weren't here tonight?"

Ray gave me a look of confusion. "Not following you, Sid," he said as he ripped off a piece of French bread and stuffed it into his mouth.

I clarified for him. "If that girl approached you tonight and I wasn't here. What do you think you would have done?"

"I would have signed her autograph."

"Then what?"

Before Ray had time to answer, a nicely dressed waiter approached the table. He was wearing a black pinstriped suit with a matching silk tie. "Good evening. I presume Mademoiselle announced this evening's special to you?" he asked in his French accent.

Ray sat forward, ready to take charge. "Yes, she did and we'll have two of the garlic roasted chicken breast and wild rice specials."

The waiter nodded and turned away to get those orders started.

I gave him a look of surprise. I'd never known Ray to take charge like that and order for me without even asking my opinion. It was kind of hot.

He shrugged and then smiled at me. "What? I've been eating with you every day since our freshman year of high school. Do you really think I don't know what you like?"

I returned his smile and realized that no matter how much time we had spent apart, we still knew each other. That was why we were so perfect together. I also couldn't refrain from being happy that he finally must have given up that ridiculous vegan diet he was on.

He sat forward again and reached for my hand, but instinctively I recoiled. I could not allow myself to fall back into his trap so easily.

I sat staring at Ray and asked him again, "After the autograph, what?"

He shook his head in annoyance, grabbed his wine glass, and gulped it down. "There would be no what, just an autograph. Now, can I just have a nice dinner with my girlfriend?"

Sitting back in my chair to widen the distance between us even further, I countered, "Well, we broke up months ago, in case you'd forgotten." Then, I pressed him once again, "What would you have done differently with that girl if I wasn't here tonight?"

He slammed his glass down on the table and leaned over as far as he could so he was whispering loudly in my ear.

"Are you asking if I would have invited her back to my hotel? Six months ago, yes, I probably would have. Once upon a time I would have, but not anymore. I told you that I'm trying to change. I'm trying to move forward with you but you're always throwing the past back in my face."

That one sentence was all it took to destroy the progress of the puzzle that was my life. Nothing had changed. Ray still possessed the ability to tear me down to my lowest level and make me cry at a moment's notice.

The waiter arrived with our food, placing the dishes down in front of us and then began topping off our wine glasses. We sat in silence, waiting for him to finish before we spoke again. Finally he finished pouring, said, "Bon appetite," bowed to us and graciously spun around on his heels to wait on the next table.

But Ray did not continue our conversation. Instead he slowly sat back in his chair, picked up his fork, and began eating like nothing had happened. I sat still, trying to control my breathing as I slowly picked up my fork, and began a feeble attempt to force the food down with the wild rice now sticking in my throat.

It had been months since we last saw each other and now that he was in front of my face, I began to doubt all of the progress I thought I had made on my own. How could it be possible to get sucked right back down into the spiral of heightened emotions and clouded judgment?

I thought I was over him. I thought I had moved on.

"My parents invited us to church tomorrow morning. Are you available?" he asked me, changing the subject.

Oh, I guess we're one big happy family again.

I reasoned if Ray was able to forgive and forget, his parents would accept me back with open arms. We would all just swing back into our normal routine and forget the fact that Ray had been arrested for slamming my head into a brick wall and let's all attend church tomorrow.

I nodded my head yes, since I was too afraid to speak in fear of what might come out. We ate the rest of our dinner in silence as I thought about Adrian's last words to me earlier that day, *"Don't let him come back this time, Sidney. You deserve better."*

After dinner we went back to the elegant hotel room that Ray's manager, Rene, had secured for him for the next week. It was absolutely amazing and I was truly impressed. But I couldn't shake the depression that was now rolling in like a heavy fog on a cold wet morning.

Ray took my hand and pulled me onto the bed. I sat there, numbly staring at the wall, still too upset to speak to him. He rested his blond head against my shoulder, looking up at me, giving me those sad puppy dog eyes.

"I'm sorry, Sid. Sometimes you can be so intense and I don't know how to handle it. I shouldn't have lost it like that. I know you're trying but I'm trying too. Sometimes it seems like you forget that part. I love you and I want you back. I know I messed up with Lilly and I'll be apologizing for that for the rest of my life. I only want to be with you."

He could see by my face that I wasn't buying it. He got up and walked across the room and took a seat at the massive oak desk.

"Do you remember when we first met?"

I nodded, "Yeah, Mr. Roman's math class freshman year."

"Technically that's when we met, but I noticed you that first day of school in the lower parking lot. You were getting out of your granny's Toyota Sequoia. Your hair was straight and you were wearing it long, down your back with one of those elastic headband thingies. You were dressed in a pale green cardigan sweater and light blue skinny jeans with those ugly boots that your friends all wore."

I was more than a little impressed. "How do you remember that?"

Ray pointed to his temple. "Because that image of you was seared into my mind forever. You were the most beautiful girl I had ever seen. I was just some nerdy twerp that hadn't hit a growth spurt yet. I believed I didn't stand a chance with you.

"That day I looked all over the campus for you. Every time I entered one of the classrooms I'd scan the entire area looking for that pale green sweater. Just when I had all but given up, there you were in my same seventh period math class."

I chimed in, "That's when we met."

He suddenly looked like he did that first day we met when he added, "Yeah, officially, but like I said, Sid. I loved you before then."

His words and the expression on his face hit me hard. But was it love at first sight? No way.

I challenged him, "Why did it take you so long to ask me out?"

We hadn't started dating right away, not until the summer going into our junior year. Every summer Ray's family would take a trip up to their cabin outside of Tahoe and on one particular trip, Ray had asked me to join him. I never thought it was strange to be invited on a week-long family vacation with a young man because he wasn't just any boy; he was my best friend. Granny knew that we were inseparable and so she never blinked an eye when I asked if I could join the Rykers on their trip.

It was an August night and the day had been excruciatingly hot and we had spent most of our time in the water until the sun had gone down. His sisters and parents had already retreated into the cabin for the night and so it had just been the two of us splashing and laughing.

Going into our junior year, Ray had changed significantly from a short, scrawny tow-headed boy to a tall, muscular young man. He now stood almost six feet tall with broad shoulders and a strong chest. He was starting to get super-hot, and I wasn't the only one to notice.

That was the same summer the boys formed their band. At first, Chrissy and I were their biggest fans but it didn't take long before Ray had a growing flock of supporters, mostly girls, who were dying to gain his attention.

When we had finally climbed out of the water and headed back to the family cabin, I had somehow managed to step on a wad of gum that had collected all sorts of debris from the woods, causing me to track it all the way onto the pinewood floors of the cabin.

I was heartbroken because they were my brand new shoes that I was supposed to be saving for the beginning of the school year, and despite Granny's warnings, I foolishly wore them to the summer retreat.

Ray sat on his bed for the next half hour, picking off every piece of sticky gum with a toothpick.

"Seriously, Sid, it's like there's a science experiment growing on the bottom of this shoe."

I sat next to him, my chin resting on his shoulder, watching his hands nimbly work to remove the mess.

I blurted out my opinion on the mess, "Blame your sister. She was the one chomping her big horse mouth on that gum all day. Doesn't Kendall know what a trash bin is?"

Ray handed me my shoe as good as new. I was so happy that I threw both of my arms around him and gave him the biggest hug as a smile beamed across my face. I looked longingly into his eyes and before I could say another word he grabbed the back of my head and pulled my face to his.

We kissed for what seemed like an eternity, causing the entire world to stand still, at least in my mind. At that moment, we were no longer in a tiny cabin tucked away in the woods. There were no longer any shouts and laughter coming from the kitchen where the rest of the family gathered. There was nothing else in the universe that mattered. It was just Ray and me, in our own private world, kissing.

He and I embraced each other, caressing, touching, and welcoming the scent and emotion that carried back and forth between us. With that first kiss, our worlds merged together, then and forever. Our lips had been so full of passion that it was no wonder we had jumped into a relationship head on and rode it like a pipeline wave.

"I wanted to kiss you like that for two years," he said, bringing me back to reality. "We hung out every day. What took you so long to notice me?"

I shot back, "What took *you* so long?"

He summed himself up honestly, "Did you see me back then? I was like the invisible kid. Not one girl wished and dreamed that I would ask her out. I was the kid that would be her worst nightmare if I asked her to the Homecoming dance."

"You took *me* to the Homecoming dance," I answered angrily, feeling truly offended.

He weakly nodded. "Yeah, and you probably went with me out of obligation for our friendship."

I shook my head. "I guess none of that stuff matters anymore. I mean, look at you now."

"That's exactly my point, Sid. Back then, before I had a band, I was just Ray Ryker who couldn't get a girl to notice him in the hallways. But now I'm Ray Ryker the lead singer of Unspoken Words. Now, all these girls flock to me, throwing themselves at me and it's like my alter ego comes out and I'm this ridiculous rock god who just wants to hook up with any hot chick I meet."

I winced. *Another punch to the gut.*

Feeling how much pain those last words brought me, I grabbed my purse and fumbled around in search for my pain killers. It looked like I still needed them after all.

I simply answered, "*I* wanted you when you were just Ray Ryker."

Ray got up and crossed the room, taking a seat next to me on the edge of the bed. "I know, Sid, and that's why when I'm with you, I am that guy. I'm that faithful, loving boyfriend that you met in freshman math class."

"But you weren't faithful, and goddammit, you weren't single, either, Ray. You're not two different people. You can't claim to be one person when you're with me and another when we're apart. That's just a cop out to defend the fact that you're still a selfish jerk!"

I stood up to leave, realizing this meeting was a mistake. But he grabbed my wrist and begged me with his eyes to stay.

After a few moments of silently debating whether I should stay or go. I made the decision to hear him out. But I also decided that I would not so easily put down my guard.

I took a step closer to him and began, "I think we should just take it slow, maybe remain friends and re-evaluate the situation in a few months."

I could see the disappointment wash over his face. I could also see the anger rising in his eyes due to the fact he was not receiving the results he wanted. He whimpered, "I thought you loved me."

I sat in silence for what seemed like an eternity. I opened my mouth but nothing came out. The truth was I *did* love him. But that was before that fateful night at the bar. And I didn't want to give Adrian up. I could never leave him when he'd been so supportive to me when I needed him. I stood in Ray's hotel room rationalizing things in my brain. Even if Ray and I got back together, Adrian and I could still be friends. I wanted to believe that.

I looked down at Ray who was now hunched over on the bed, running his hands through his blond hair. Finally, he sat up and met my gaze. I was shocked to see that same look he had that night at the bar. Fear began shooting through my soul.

"You're still seeing him, aren't you? That's why you don't want to get back together."

Okay, so maybe Adrian and I would not be able to remain friends.

Attempting to defuse the situation, I reached over and took his hand again. "You're right, Ray. I do love you and nothing's changed."

Why did this guy make me so stupid? Was I still a freshman, here?

He squeezed it tight, searching my face for the truth, and he must have been pleased with what he saw because I watched as the fire in his eyes burned out and was replaced with the smoldering look of lust. He grabbed my face and pulled me down next to him, kissing me passionately. I closed my eyes and gave in to the swirls of ecstasy surrounding me. The room started spinning as I lost myself in him.

He pulled his head back slightly and I opened my eyes. He tenderly whispered, "Thank you for giving me another chance. I promise I won't blow it this time."

We kissed again and I knew what he said was true. Ray broke away from our kiss and flashed me a big smile of his perfect white teeth. Then, like a little boy he exclaimed, "I have a surprise for you. Let's go downstairs.

* * *

We entered the double doors to the hotel ballroom and all at once it was as if we had been transported into a parallel universe. The place was dark except for the different strobe lights flashing every which way and my ears were flooded by the thunderous music being played on what seemed to be a full-sized arena stage.

The beat was a cheerful tune that immediately made me want to dance and the song sounded vaguely familiar.

My face lit up at the familiarity of the band. "Is this The Neon—"

Ray smiled knowingly and nodded his head as he cut me off in midsentence. "We've been opening for them on tour. Tyler and I have become pretty close. He agreed to sing at the event tonight."

It was surreal to hear Ray on a first name basis with one of the hottest bands in the country, but it reflected the status Ray had attained.

"What kind of event is this?" I asked, still getting used to the visual spectacle.

Ray placed his arm around my shoulders and pulled me close as we walked into the festivities. "The radio station here in San Francisco wanted to throw us a post-award party. It's their way to congratulate us for winning the 'Best Breakthrough Band' award."

A nicely dressed man holding a tray of the most luxurious bottled water I had ever seen approached us. Ray grabbed one as he gave the man a nod of appreciation. Once the man was out of earshot, Ray looked at me and said in the deepest, most sophisticated voice, "Would you like to purify yourself with the waters of Lake Minnetonka?"

I buried my face in his shoulder and tried to stifle my laughter. Ray's mom Teresa was a huge Prince fan and Ray loved to make fun of his movie *Purple Rain* at his mother's expense.

He shouted, "Come on, let's dance."

Before I had time to answer, Ray was pulling me out on the floor and we were dancing as one of my favorite bands sang less than five feet away. The whole thing felt more than a little surreal, as if I could blink and all of this could disappear. I held on to Ray as we both laughed, and sang, and danced, just like old times.

Ray may have outshone me on all other aspects of life, but on the dance floor, I was the Queen. After all, I was the one who taught *him* how to dance at Homecoming years before.

After a few songs, we tirelessly left the dance floor in search of some of that purifying water. Ray led me over to the bar and asked me to wait for him while he went to use the bathroom. I ordered two waters and went to take a seat at a nearby table. Then, I heard my name being called.

"Sidney Sinclair? Is that really you or are my eyes deceiving me?"

I knew that flat, dry voice anywhere. I plastered a fake smile on my face and spun around as graciously as I could.

"Rene! It's been a long time," I responded with my excellent brand of fake enthusiasm.

The thin, blonde woman stood erect in a black skintight dress as she held a dirty martini in the air. Her hair was just as I remembered, straight and shoulder length with bangs cut across her forehead in a razor straight line. Her big sunglasses were replaced with an even bigger pair of fake eyelashes.

She stabbed the olive with her drink stirrer and plopped it into her mouth. Swallowing it down, she answered, "It certainly has. I was expecting it to be a little longer, given the last publicity nightmare we had to go through on your behalf. The P.R. team has been making it their mission to make sure Ray didn't break down and call you." She frowned slightly before continuing, "I might have to fire them."

Rene's insulting words actually relieved me. To hear that Ray hadn't contacted me in six months because the label restricted him meant it wasn't *his* decision to stay away from me.

He didn't hate me after all.

Gulping down her martini, Rene continued, "Of course I'm not surprised to see you. The love you two have for each other doesn't die easily. Let's just try to refrain from any more drunken bar fights, okay? Water's probably the safest choice for both of you."

And then she was gone, leaving me standing, mouth open, staring at the two bottles of water I was holding.

Rene was a bitch but I think there was a bit of a compliment in what she had said to me. She had just validated that what Ray and I have, is in fact, special.

Ray reappeared and I handed him his water. He took a swig of it and was ready to pull me back onto the dance floor but then Chrissy and Finn came into view. I let go of Ray's hand and ran over to my best friend.

I had to ask them, "How's everything going?"

Finn put his arm around Chrissy's shoulders and answered, "Oh you know. We're making progress but it would go a lot faster if I had a jack hammer to break this ice."

Chrissy brushed his arm off her and pursed her lips at him. "You call *this* progress, Finn Aldman? Progress will be made when you tell your jerk of a cousin never to sing that song again!"

Ray came up behind me and wrapped his arms around my waist and laughed at Chrissy and Finn's dramatic tone. "Oh please, Chrissy, you know you love every second of this," Ray joked.

Finn bellowed, "She sure does. She loves it so much she's going to take me back, isn't that right, doll face?"

Before Chrissy could respond, Finn grabbed her head and planted a big kiss on her cheek.

Chrissy put a finger in his face and warned, "You keep those lips away from me and I am not your doll face, got it?"

Of course, we all knew that Chrissy's bark was louder than her bite. Her eyes were glowing and she *was* enjoying every moment.

Ray began to kiss my neck and then moved his lips to my ear and whispered, "Can we go someplace to talk?"

I nodded, and we turned and snuck away from the two undercover love birds.

This night was amazingly perfect but we both knew we still had a lot of unfinished business. After we had exited the double doors, we took a seat on a small bench in the hotel lobby.

"Look, Ray…" I began, but Ray cut me off before I could finish.

"No, Sid. Let me start. I want you to know that I didn't mean any of those things I said to you that night."

He put his hand on my forehead and rubbed my small scar. "And most importantly, I didn't mean to push you. That was the stupidest mistake of my life. I drank way too much and it just brought the devil out in me."

I cringed at his choice of words. There was something about Ray and his faith that still bothered me. Or, perhaps it was just Adrian's *lack* of faith rubbing off of me. God, The Devil, all of that tomfoolery was just an excuse for humans to act absurd. Religion was not my strong suit.

"I was so friggin' stupid," Ray continued. "I know that you never would cheat on me. I was obviously just feeling guilty about my own actions and I tried to turn it around on you. It wasn't fair to you, and I'm sorry for that, Sid."

"I'm sorry too, Ray. I've thought about you every day and you don't know how badly I've wanted things to go back to normal."

His eyes shot up in anticipation of what I was going to say.

"But what is normal, Ray? It hasn't been normal since high school."

He had no answer for that one. We sat in silence. He knew I was right. But what could we do about it? It's not like he was going to quit his band.

"I made a promise to you, Sid, and I'm going to keep my word." He met my eyes with a look of confidence and determination.

I sat in disbelief.

Was Ray telling me that he wanted to come back into my life forever?

I didn't want to hear any more of his empty promises. I didn't want to cling to an imaginary rope of hope. I slipped my hand out of his grip and sat back on the bench, lost in thought.

"What are you thinking?" he asked me, too afraid to make eye contact.

I got to the heart of the matter. "I don't want to be given a false sense of hope just to be disappointed again."

He hesitated, drinking down his bottle of water before answering, then he delivered his bombshell.

Suddenly, he was kneeling in front of me. He pulled a black velvet box out of his pocket and opened his mouth to speak. Ray did speak but I didn't hear a word of it. All I could hear was a high pitched ringing in my ears as the room began to spin. I felt nauseous as I gripped my stomach and focused on holding my food down.

I looked at Ray, he was staring up at me, waiting for an answer to the question I didn't hear. But the open box told me all I needed to know. Inside that tiny case was a beautiful, vintage-looking ring. The center held a humongous diamond solitaire and the rest of the band was splattered with tiny blue sapphires.

"You told me you didn't want a new necklace, so I decided to take it a step further and ask you. Will you marry me?"

I hesitated. I didn't know how to answer. I didn't know whether to believe this was really happening.

"Ray, our relationship has been nothing but a struggle. We always come close to happiness, but we never reach it."

He smiled boldly, "I'll struggle for you until I take my last breath, Sidney Sinclair."

I flinched at the use of my full name, he was dead serious.

"Since that night of my arrest, there has been a pictorial timeline of my life in the spotlight. Never once have I been photographed with another girl. There's been no one since that night because I've realized that I love only you. I'm nothing without you."

Instantly my mind was thrust back into the scene from *The Great Gatsby* when Tom Buchanan and Gatsby were fighting over Daisy.

I always come back to you, Daisy.

My future life began to flash before my eyes of what it would be like if I accepted Ray's proposal: the big house with the lonely walls imprisoning me in a life of sadness and regret. The empty life that Daisy had felt would be transferred to me. If Ray and I decided to have a family, would he be there for the birth, the first words, the first baby steps or would he be constantly on tour being idolized by his millions of fans? I would be alone, just like Daisy had been as she dreamt about being with Gatsby.

The last thought took my breath away and I finally saw what Adrian had tried to make me see the night we watched the film.

Besides, I don't have a Gatsby pining after me, purchasing a mansion next to my house for me to live in.

It hit me.

Holy shit, Adrian is my Gatsby!

I jumped up from the bench and scanned the lobby, looking for the nearest escape plan as my track and field instincts kicked in. Ray, still down on one knee, immediately realized what my intentions were.

His eyes grew wide with the fear of rejection and he shook his head and whispered, "Please don't do this, Sid."

But I couldn't help it. My mind was reeling out of control. There was still so much left unfinished here. I needed to clear my head and I could only do that by seeing Adrian. I needed to speak with him before I could consider Ray's proposal.

I glanced down at Ray one last time, his blue eyes were glazed over and I knew that I was breaking his heart but I couldn't stop myself.

"Don't run away from me," he begged.

Ray knew me so well that it was quite possible he was my other half. But I couldn't accept a marriage to him without first talking to Adrian. I owed him that much.

Doing exactly what Ray had begged me not to do, I ran away from him.

I burst through the glass doors and ran out into the open streets of San Francisco. Immediately, I was bombarded with the flash bulbs of the paparazzi as they screamed their questions toward me.

"When's the wedding, Sidney?"

"Will you and Ray be attending couples counseling to manage your anger?"

"What if he hits you again, that was a pretty gnarly cut he left on your head the last time."

Ignoring all of these strangers' intrusive questions I continued to push my way through the mob and escaped the hotel.

It was dark and a heavy rain was pouring down on me but I didn't care. I took off my heels and held them in my hand as I raced toward the train station.

I had to see Adrian.

About the Author

Cynthia Austin is a multi-published author who lives in Northern California with her husband, two boys, and Sheepadoodle named Chowder. They love all things horror, gothic, and Victorian which prompts her friends to dub them as "The Adams Family."

She is an avid reader who may be slightly obsessed with music. She hears music in a way that she believes the artist intended it to be heard: visually, with a storyline that follows. Listening to the songs by her favorite artists, she was inspired to write her first series titled "The Pendant."

New Release Must Reads!

FROM AWARD-WINNING AUTHOR
BARBARA CASEY

**For more information
visit:** www.SpeakingVolumes.us

www.ingramcontent.com/pod-product-compliance
Lightning Source LLC
Chambersburg PA
CBHW020641130726
47903CB00003BA/940